GLIMMER TRAIN
STORIES

EDITORS
Susan Burmeister-Brown
Linda Burmeister Davies

CONSULTING EDITORS
Britney Gress
Tamara Moan
Stephen Sund
Brian Vandiver

COPY EDITOR & PROOFREADER
Scott Allie

TYPESETTING & LAYOUT
Heidi Weitz Siegel

COVER ILLUSTRATOR
Jane Zwinger

STORY ILLUSTRATOR
Jon Leon

PUBLISHED QUARTERLY
in spring, summer, fall, and winter by
Glimmer Train Press, Inc.
710 SW Madison Street, Suite 504
Portland, Oregon 97205-2900 U.S.A.
Telephone: 503/221-0836
Facsimile: 503/221-0837
www.glimmertrain.com
PRINTED IN U.S.A.
Indexed in *The American Humanities Index.*

Glimmer Train (ISSN #1055-7520), registered in U.S. Patent and Trademark Office, is published quarterly, $32 per year in the U.S., by Glimmer Train Press, Inc., Suite 504, 710 SW Madison, Portland, OR 97205. Periodicals postage paid at Portland, OR, and additional mailing offices. POSTMASTER: Send address changes to Glimmer Train Press, Inc., Suite 504, 710 SW Madison, Portland, OR 97205.

ISSN # 1055-7520, ISBN # 1-880966-25-5, CPDA BIPAD # 79021

DISTRIBUTION: Bookstores can purchase *Glimmer Train Stories* through these distributors:
Anderson News Co., 6016 Brookvale Ln., #151, Knoxville, TN 37919
Ingram Periodicals, 1226 Heil Quaker Blvd., LaVergne, TN 37086
IPD, 674 Via de la Valle, #204, Solana Beach, CA 92075
Peribo PTY Ltd., 58 Beaumont Rd., Mt. Kuring-Gai, NSW 2080, AUSTRALIA
Ubiquity, 607 Degraw St., Brooklyn, NY 11217

SUBSCRIPTION SVCS: EBSCO, Faxon, READMORE

Subscription rates: One year, $32 within the U.S. (Visa/MC/check). Airmail to Canada, $43; outside North America, $54. Payable by Visa/MC or check for U.S. dollars drawn on a U.S. bank.

Attention short-story writers: We pay $500 for first publication and onetime anthology rights. Please include a self-addressed, sufficiently stamped envelope with your submission. **Send manuscripts in January, April, July, and October.** *Send a SASE for guidelines, which will include information on our Short-Story Award for New Writers and our Very Short Fiction Award.*

Dedication

We dedicate this issue to these six men
and all the others.

World War II. After Normandy, before the end.
Left to right and around: Captain "Nick" Podlesski,
Henry Burmeister, Jacob Fuld, Helmut Kuhn, Sammy
Seif, and Walter Schmaus. One Catholic and one
Russian Orthodox, the others Jews. One gay, the
others straight. All, we guess, were loved by their
grandmothers, all dreaded killing and feared
being killed. And here they sit, six friends,
alive and smiling in the sunlight.

Linda & Susan

ONTENTS

CONTENTS

Kathryn Trueblood

Me and the Holy Ghost (age five).

Kathryn Trueblood's novella and stories, *The Sperm Donor's Daughter and Other Tales of Modern Family*, will be published by The Permanent Press in April. She has co-edited two anthologies of American multicultural literature, *The Before Columbus Foundation Fiction Anthology: Selections from the American Book Awards*, with Ishmael Reed and Shawn Wong (W.W. Norton, 1992); and *Homeground*, with Linda Stovall (Blue Heron, 1996). *Homeground* won the Jurors' Choice Award at Bumbershoot, Seattle's annual arts festival. Her stories have been published in the *Seattle Review*, the *Cimarron Review*, *Zyzzyva*, and other literary journals. Since 1991, she has taught at Western Washington University in Bellingham, where she lives with her husband and son.

KATHRYN TRUEBLOOD
One of Me Watching

*J*awakened on the train somewhere between
Amsterdam and Copenhagen feeling sunken into myself like
a fallen cake. It was the summer I met the Swedish family my
mother had married us into. I took the ferry from Copenhagen
to Malmo, the southern tip of Sweden, where I was picked up
by my eldest cousin who drove me to the summer house in the
archipelago. He played the music very loud, the volume up so
high I couldn't even hear the wind. A new English rock band,
he told me. It sounded to me like ten people beating
their forks on their dinner plates and chanting the menu.

Driving through a field of *raps* in bloom was like staring into
the sun—yellow until the very lines of your iris felt like
splinters of light around a gaping hole. For relief, I looked
across the North Sea at the heavy clouds that brooded over
Denmark and the hard slate color of the water. Everything
seemed brilliant or hard.

Lillasundholmen, island in the little straits, is where I arrived.
My mother and Kjell, her new husband, were staying on his
boat next to the dock. Above it on a hill sat the big house
beneath the birch trees. Like the other buildings on the island,
the house was a burnished red, its paint a by-product of a

method of copper mining long gone. The property was
bordered by a fjord, beyond it the forest full of sounds feathery
and hissing.

I was reading on deck, waiting for the rest of the family to
come down for the day's sailing excursion—lying on my
stomach because I couldn't get used to the idea of these new
relatives seeing me without my top on. I couldn't get used to
the idea of having breasts at all. Every time I looked down, I
noticed the space between them.

I made my palms into fists and stacked them one on top of
the other, resting my chin in the cavity. From this vantage
point, I could see everyone on shore whose names I didn't
remember yet. My two uncles were inspecting the broken
rigging of one of the children's boats. My aunts sat together on
the steps of the cabin by the shore, stripping dill, topping beets,
and talking. Over the side of the bow, I could see my cousins
as they plummeted down into the clear water.

I got up and went to sit above the galley doorway, hanging
my feet down over it. "Hand me my T-shirt," I said to my
mother, who was fixing coffee in the cabin.

"Hasn't anyone ever told you that it's not polite to hang your
feet from the kitchen ceiling?" she said, grabbing hold of my
swinging legs by the ankles.

"So what," I said. "Nobody cares if you eat naked here
either."

I looked at Kjell sleeping. Beneath his mustache, his mouth
was small and pursed like a kitten's—fine tilting lines at either
side. My mother was watching him too. She stroked her cheek
with the tail of her thick braid.

It was a signal I knew; Kjell must have been a good lover. I
looked at his feet—narrow and bony and in no way warped.

"Kjell has sweet feet," I said to my mother. She came up from
the galley, slapping my calves as she emerged.

"You like him better now, don't you?"

8   *Glimmer Train Stories*

"I always did like him," I said, which was true. She stood below me, leaning over the hatch and resting her crossed arms on my knees. I tucked a stray hair behind her ear.

"You don't think I'd do wrong by you, do you?" she asked.

"You left Daddy," I said and shrugged.

"Yes, I did. I left him and he dove to the bottom of a scotch bottle, which is where he was headed anyway. All my fault, huh?"

"I didn't say that," I told her ruefully, wishing I could back-pedal my way out of what I'd started.

"It's not always what people say, you know. No one ever says a bad word about your father. It's because he has a mean streak a mile wide." With that, she pressed my legs and stood back.

"Maybe that's where I got it," I said.

She gave me her hawk-like scanning look. "Maybe," she said, going down into the galley.

Back on shore, my grandfather and Anders were making their way down to the dock. Moggens's body frame was massive, and I saw in his careful determined movements a latent power. I'm sure he would have liked to pick his disabled brother up, carry him under one arm and the ambulator under the other. I jumped down from my perch and stuck my head in the galley.

"I'm sorry, Mother," I said.

"It's all right, Frances," she said wearily, and I felt that I had spoiled her mood.

"Did I wreck everything?" I asked.

She came up the stair level with me, and gently put her fist to my cheek. "If it were that easy to wreck my everything, then it wasn't much to begin with. No, baby, you didn't."

"Moggens and Anders are coming now," I said.

"Well good," she said, "then we'll only have to wait another half century."

We stood very close without touching and listened to the halyards ring out against the mast. I took the tail of her braid and wrapped it around my thumb. We were both looking at Kjell, asleep in the sun.

"Watch this," my mother whispered. "Kjell," she said in her melodic voice. He smiled a little but did not wake.

"Do it again," I said.

"Kjell," my mother repeated even more softly—and again the gentle smile. She sighed. "I hate to wake him."

"*Kjell!* " I shouted. He sat straight up and fixed us with his granite gray eyes.

"You rat," my mother said laughing, and then to Kjell in her most soothing tones, "We thought you'd like coffee."

"You see," I said, turning to follow her, "he doesn't love *me.*"

On Kjell's forty-fifth birthday, an hour before we were due at the party, I sat with my mother on the pier, my back against her knees. As we discussed what I would wear, she braided my hair, gathering the stray strands with soft strokes while keeping the plait between the thumb and forefinger of her other hand. I felt the reflection of the sun on the water in the flush of my face and watched the light in the reeds as it shifted between the ridged blades. My mother was talking and I dozed, my eyelashes dividing the fjord in bands of shadow.

"I couldn't ever have afforded to send you to art school at home, or to graduate school for that matter, if you decide later that's what you want. Of course you'll have to start the government Swedish classes soon, but that won't be a problem for you."

My mother liked to believe in me. I was her vehicle of faith. "You can do anything, Frances," she often told me, "anything at all," as though she hadn't had the same option. If I were to have said that she made some choices along the way, she would have reminded me of the letters that supposedly came every Christmas from my father's lawyer, threatening to take her to court, threatening to take me away; and it was this she told me that kept her from going back to school, that kept her at the job she didn't like. I don't remember my parents' divorce, and I never saw the letters.

According to my mother, there were no limitations on my happiness. I could get my Ph.D. if I wanted, become a brilliant professor or museum curator or psychiatrist—all the things she thought she might have been good at. And then I could glow in the knowledge of having rectified her mistakes. My mother picked men like dandelions and blew the hot rage of her unsatisfied wishes on them until they scattered like seed.

The party in celebration of Kjell's forty-fifth birthday was at Krista and Murre's house across the fjord. Kjell's childhood friends came around the house to the backyard where the tables had been set beneath the trees. They came carrying between them a string of candy and singing.

I ended up in the kitchen with Krista and Murre where I asked Murre what he did, and he told me that he sold casters for office furniture. "The little metal balls," he said, making a circle with thumb and forefinger, shrugging and smiling as if to imply that he'd long ago accepted that there wasn't much to say about it. He fished a cigar out of his pocket, poked it playfully at Krista's ribs, and left the clamor of the women who were assembling in the kitchen.

Krista gave me some cucumbers to peel, and after making a sound of annoyance in her throat, explained to me in English, "He smokes cigars all day. In the morning, he spits in the sink, doesn't bother to wash it away." She poured a heavy cream over a casserole of fish in a glass pan and, as we watched the cream rise over the shiny filets, she continued to vent her outrage. "He wears a gun around the house sometimes too, thinks he is John Wayne, the barrel shoved in the waistband of his pants, my God!"

To me, Murre looked as though he might have been as tall as his wife when he was twenty-two, but years of telephone sales had caused his spine to sink. The roll around his midriff was such that standing up, he couldn't possibly have pressed his groin against her. I saw that when he came in and kissed her, a smooch so loud I knew it must have been for my benefit. Krista had a loose eye, like a fish in a round bowl, magnified and looming one instant, the next sliding away. I finished peeling the cucumbers but left them uncut by the sink.

I didn't see anywhere to sit in the living room so I stood by the door. My great-uncle, Anders, was the only other person standing, leaning against the far wall by the dining-room table. His face had the look of a jack-o'-lantern abandoned on the back porch, smiling crookedly into a swirl of leaves, and slumping further. His eyes too, it seemed, bore the weight of rotten pulp, though it was booze and cigarettes that had swelled his lids so that they hung down into his field of vision. And no one in the family was quite sure what Anders's field of vision included. My grandfather, Moggens, had explained to me that when Anders looked at your face, he saw only your shoulders, but that when he looked above your head, he saw your head. I had gotten used to him staring at the air above my head. From the change in his expressions when we talked, I knew that was where he saw my face.

The faces of Kjell's friends were marked by weariness, not striving—good faces all the same. His friends were people who had made themselves content with what they had found, who hadn't gone far looking for it. They asked about Kjell's travels, becoming both intimidated and jealous, and marveled at how he had retained his youthful looks. "People who keep the world running," my mother said of his friends, "the ones we should be grateful to for keeping home the same." I didn't know what she could have meant by that for us, considering the number of places we'd lived, but my grandparents still lived in the house where she was born, and I almost could have found their faces at that party, if I'd looked.

My mother was waving to me across the room, and I headed dutifully in her direction, steeling myself for another round of introductions. Everyone kept telling me how lucky I was, as though I'd been waiting my whole life to become Kjell's step-daughter. They didn't know what else to say. They wanted to see if I was nice, and they hoped Kjell wasn't unlucky for having gotten a package deal. I was very nice. It didn't mean anything. Social pleasantries are like worry beads: everyone fidgeting with them incessantly, clacking them together.

I drifted into the dining room where a group of men were sitting at the table discussing the economy or cars; I couldn't tell which because the only words I recognized were Volvo, Saab, and *huit*, the latter being the Swedish word for shit, close in sound to its English counterpart and said with the same vehemence. I looked at my grandfather's cigarettes on the table. I knew I should stop stealing from him and just ask for one in private.

I liked going to find Moggens, alone in his study. As we talked, he'd rub his eye with his thumb while holding a cigarette between his first two fingers, from time to time singeing his fore-lock but too intent on the conversa-tion to be much troubled by it. He was the one I knew to ask for Anders's

J. LEON 97-

story, the one who told me that Marthe was the name of Anders's wife—headstrong, young Marthe, who took her daughter to swim in the rough waters on the west coast. Anders tried to rescue them, one under each arm, then one lost, Anders not knowing which it was. That's when his head met the rock and his wife went to sea. That's how he got the brain hemorrhage.

Moggens caught my questioning glance—I was trying to figure out how to make off with one of his cigarettes—and mistook it for curiosity. The men at the table were still laughing over a joke he'd just finished. "Come over here," he called, "come over and I'll tell you."

"Yes," my uncle Hasse said, wiping his eyes, "tell her the King of the Shit House story."

"Ah, now you've ruined it." Moggens exclaimed, dropping both hands to the table.

"No he hasn't," I insisted, "tell me." I leaned against Moggens's chair and he put his arms around my hips.

"Well, once there was a maintenance man for apartment buildings, and as extra work on holidays—you understand this man worked all the time—he worked at the train-station bathroom. This fellow, he was a very straight fellow, never let bums loiter or slide down walls, never was afraid to approach drunks or toughs, never even considered being afraid ..."

"And me," my uncle interjected, hitting himself in the chest with his thumb, "I become a professional so the government can take eighty percent."

My grandfather put up his hand at which Hasse downed his schnapps and grunted.

"So one day the railway-station manager approached this man because he'd heard that the government was accepting bids on the leasing of the bathrooms. 'No,' the man said, 'they would never choose me,' but his wife, she forces him to put in a bid, and he gets it. So now he makes ... oh, two hundred thousand *kroner* a year in black money."

"Who can count the coins for the toilet!" my uncle roared.

"And," Moggens continued, "he is by our standards a millionaire. In the United States, you have movie stars. In Sweden, the King of the Shit House gets rich!"

At this, the men chuckled, except of course my uncle, who was rapping his knuckles on the table. I smiled and squeezed Moggens's shoulder, but I had only been half-listening, the rest of my attention on Anders, who stood against the wall on the other side of the room.

While Moggens had been telling his story, Anders's mouth had been working, forming words he couldn't get out. I moved to him, leaned over his ambulator, and ran my hand across his forehead, pressing down the veins that had risen there. He closed his mouth, and as he smiled his eyelids drooped with the release of the strain.

The men at the table resumed their discussion. I heard the word Electrolux mentioned several times. Anders seemed to be listening, though he stared steadily at me. He curled his fingers and very deliberately made a tunnel of his hand. When he was sure my attention was fixed on it, he dropped his hand to his crotch and made a loud, wet, sucking sound, saying quite clearly and with exaggerated satisfaction: "Electrolux ... my first woman." The moment after he said it, he shook his head as if to deny it, and then he grinned. I laughed so hard with him it made me weak, and I hung on to the other side of his ambulator until I felt my mother's eyes on me.

That night at the dinner table, I chose to sit next to Anders; he was the only person I could supply with words. He would lose words he wanted and become reconnected to others he didn't want.

"I want the tomatoes," he said. So I passed him the tomatoes. He shook his head. "I want," he paused, "the tomato." I took the spoon, believing that he wanted a slice of tomato, and served him. He slumped further into his chair and began again. "I want," he said, and pointed, I thought, at the fruit basket.

"Ah," I said, "the fruit." He was still pointing, so I took an apple and a banana from the basket. He took the apple from my hand.

"An apple," he said slowly, marveling at its shape and the feel of the word on his tongue. Then nodding at me in encouragement, he spoke in Swedish and waited for my response.

So I repeated the words to him, making my best effort at pronunciation. "*Jag har ett apple och en banan.*"

"*Jah,*" he said with the sharp intake of breath particular to Swedish inflection.

"*Jah,*" I answered, and in the end we both considered that we had done rather well.

By early evening, the party had moved to the backyard where the children were playing soccer. I saw my mother at the water pump and noticed how pretty she'd become since we'd moved to Sweden. She was wearing one of Kjell's shirts, the tail of it outlining her ample rump rather nicely. Kjell was often patting her there, when she leaned over to peer into the oven or to spit toothpaste into the sink. He wasn't a rump slapper like her last boyfriend, and I didn't think I'd ever wake to find him breathing over my bed. Now we called her last boyfriend "bog breath" and "mouth breather," when we mentioned him at all.

Krista and Murre were out on the driveway. He'd come back from making a run to the store for sugar, and she'd been clipping flowers. She stood by the car, one arm dangling with the weight of the shears. He hung his arms over the open door and his bad air blew into her wispy hair. From the look on his face, she'd just told him that in all the time they'd known each other, he'd been rubbing her clitoris backwards. She strode off, carrying the flowers, blooms down, in a stranglehold. He slammed the door, eyeing the men in the yard with the bottle between them, wondering how in hell you figure out what is frontwards and backwards of a thing not shaped for travel anyway, bow and stern, yes. Yes, I'm sure he suddenly yearned to be out on his boat, which unlike his wife would signal the first moment of miscalculation. And me, I yearned to be away from all these people—away where my imagination would not have the chance to give meaning to conversations I scarcely understood a word of.

I walked quickly into the forest at the edge of the garden. Birch, aspen, oak, and spruce vied to turn their leaves in the sun, to display their own variant of green, and the forest floor was laced with leaves like interlocking fingers. The sun was slinking behind a veil of cloud. In the sudden damp of the woods, I felt stricken at having left my mother alone back there. But it crossed my mind then, too, that it was me that felt alone in the midst of my new family, not her.

I remembered the day before my mother left for Sweden, and I for my grandparents'. We stayed in bed all morning, reading magazines, letting the phone ring, filling out a computer-dating application together. I read aloud to her: "If none of the answers following a particular question is the exact answer you wish to give, then mark the answer that comes closest." The vase of flowers I'd put on her breakfast tray fell over, and when finally she stopped laughing, she told me it was true—that most of her friends had given up on finding the *right* man and picked the man that came closest. The friends that kept looking also kept marrying. I asked her if that was true of her, and she winced, as though I had made a loud noise or pulled the shade up.

"Maybe," she said, "but that's over now."

The application listed thinking as an activity right along with hiking, sailing, and skiing. I told her I would check only that box. I said it to cheer her up, but I would have done just that, and waited to see who I got. It was the closest I could come to a mystery box.

Once out of the forest, I walked along a path through the marsh grass until I came to a beach where I saw a row of bathhouses, all of them boarded up. I knocked at the first one anyway and saw myself as in a dream: one of me watching, one of me doing. The other of me stepped lightly from the bathhouse in a black, knee-length bathing suit with bloomers, and a silk bathing cap adorned with a pink rosette.

"And who will go for a swim with me?" she shouted, and when she saw that the beach was empty, she disappeared.

I knocked at the next bathhouse and saw the door fly open so forcibly it banged against the side of the building, and myself in seven layers of raw linen and a waistband of gold and serpentine, my hair bound by a sinew of green willow.

"Where is his ship?" she shouted, and when she saw that the sea was empty, she disappeared.

I didn't bother to knock at the next bathhouse, and the only version of me that wouldn't disappear ground a deep pivot in the sand with her heel and headed for the stretch of beach where all sign of humanity had long since been erased by pattern of wind and wave. I was drawing on the air with the tip of a feather when I saw a bolt of silver break the water, and Anders emerge, shedding light droplets from his shoulders, opening his fingers skyward. Young, lean, smiling at me, he dove. And I waited. I waited for the longest time. Then I walked 'til I imagined I was just a speck of the girl that had started off.

All the phrases in Swedish that I no longer wanted in my head and which were never there when I needed them kept busting in on my thoughts. *Nei tac, jog har en kupp kaffe just innen jog komma hite.* No thank you, I had a cup of coffee just before I came here. I said the phrases aloud and after a while was rid of them, content to concentrate on the hum of the wind against the white feather in my hand.

Kjell was nearly abreast of me before I heard the soles of his feet squeak against the sand. He was red in the face from exertion, and his eyes radiated such fierce concern I couldn't look at him. It was as though I'd never seen him before, as though he'd been a rock to me, and I'd thought to myself whenever I saw him, That rock is boring black and white; but then the sun had emerged from behind a cloud and picked up all the tiny particles of mica in the stone and thrown their light like glitter in the air.

I stared at our bare feet in the sand, both of us making furrows with our toes. I stared at our feet hard, in expectation, hoping to find clues in the conversation our toes were having for the one we should start.

When finally Kjell had gotten his breath, he asked, "Are you all right, Frances? Why did you leave?"

I looked up at him then and felt something hideous rising from the bottom of my stomach, some gargantuan beast about to crash and heave through the underbrush. "I hate your friends!" I shouted.

He let me breathe a while after that. I had to. The tears that came to my eyes flowed fast and freely no matter how I mopped at them with the cuff of my sweater. He reached out to touch my face, but I pulled away.

"Let's walk," he said quietly, turning towards the house.

We both looked at the water, listening to the gentle overlap of waves and the accompanying motif our footfalls made.

"I'm sorry," I said at last.

He shrugged, appearing aggravated, and said, "You don't have to be. I've known them all forever, and I've hated each and every one of them at a different time."

I looked at him, incredulous.

"No, it's true," he said, looking away. "I went to Tunisia once with Jonas and Birgitta, on vacation, except there was a flood, and the two of them, Jesus, they sat around in the hotel room drinking all day and sulking like babies. And Roger, he got fat since I went to the States, and turned chicken shit, sold his sailboat for a motor boat. And Krista, what a case, seeing a psychiatrist three times a week, all the time telling everybody she wants to divorce Murre but she's too afraid. Then when they go on vacation, she threatens to jump overboard and kill herself."

"You're kidding."

"No, I'm not," he said, "and I could tell you worse."

"Well then who do you like?" I blurted out.

We stopped before the dark tunnel of trees that led back to the house, and when he turned his eyes towards me, I was stunned again by their brilliance, but I didn't look away.

"Like," he said slowly, contemplating the meaning of the word.

"No one, but your mother I love, and love is all the time; then the rest doesn't matter so much."

Lena, my grandmother, said Anders couldn't walk without the four-pronged ambulator, but I found out it wasn't true. One morning I woke at three and saw the sun rising, trailing yellow streamers all across the sky. I knew it would stay that way for hours, that I could turn my back on the moment I longed to savor, and when I turned 'round again, it would still be there—the light just the same. I went downstairs to the front room with its big windows. The ducks were barking the way they do with too much water in their gullets. Then I heard Anders's door open and the terrible crashing that followed.

Before he could get a foot in front of him, his upper body fell forward. At that moment, he slammed a hand flat on the wall and with the retrograde motion, threw one of his legs out. Although older than Moggens, he had no fear of brittle bones. He wrapped his arms around corners and reached for walls as though they were rings to swing by.

When finally he saw me sitting on the couch, he smiled his side-sagging smile, and, leaning over his left foot, he took a huge step with his right. His gait was like that of a child at the age when walking is a precarious gathering of momentum. Watching him, I felt the earth did not go around evenly at all.

I got up and took his arm, and using me instead of the walls to swing towards and away from, he made his way to the couch. We sat and watched the low hummocks of islands come up off the flat horizon as the sun struck them. We watched the light running down the filament of the fish nets stretched out on the rack beside the docks; the air itself like them, full of light droplets running down trajectories. Very suddenly, he touched my cheek.

"Marthe," he said softly.

Without thinking, I answered, "No, I'm not Marthe, I'm Frances," and then I saw him wince. And then I knew it wasn't simply a word he'd lost.

During *Kräftskiva*, the feast in celebration of the early fall and the coming of the small, red crawdads, I sucked dill butter and brine from between spiny legs before cracking open the *kräfta* with my thumbs. Red was the color of the season: bright change against new cold. The ronne berries on the windowsill were the same color as the crawfish we ate, as the ladybugs I shook off the quilt before bringing it in from the line, as the cherry juice on my mother's lips. We picked the last of the cherries together in the orchard behind the house.

"Imagine," my mother said, "the people who lived here made everything, from the garden to the fishnets. And now we're so worried about becoming specialists."

"Mom, the pioneers did everything too," I reminded her.

"Exactly," she said, smiling gaily, the basket of cherries balanced in the crook of her arm. She had a way of assuming anything I said to the favor of her argument—that it might have been a challenge didn't occur to her. I kept wondering how I could be so hateful. "Look," I wanted to say, "it's not all that unique here." But I knew what she would say, and I knew it was no alternative. So did she, which is why she would have told me, "You can go live with your father if you don't like life with me."

I didn't push it because I didn't want to hear that ultimatum again, and I didn't want to be fixing Bloody Marys for my father on Sunday mornings. Besides, I was just thinking how much I was getting to like my room with its wallpaper of blue corn flowers and the wood-burning stove and the fir bench with a straight back like a church pew and the foot-pedal organ—even how much I was beginning to like Kjell and the smell of fresh wood shavings in his mustache when he kissed me good morning.

Back in the kitchen, I watched the cherries tumble from my mother's basket into the colander. She handled them with care, and they glistened in the water like dark rubies. My grand-mother was sifting flour for a cake while outside Kjell made a saw sing across the boards he'd measured to fix the roof. He came in to drink and stopped for a moment behind my mother. He dangled a cherry by its stem above her head, like a lure on a line, and she went up on her toes after it. I could hear them laughing as I snuck up the stairs to my grandparents' quarters.

My new grandmother was demented about her dogs—pictures of her two dachshunds right up there on the wall alongside her real grandchildren, both dogs with that stricken look common to most non-poisonous bat-boned creatures. And Lena was kind. At each new moon, she bent her knees three times and made a wish. And all the wishes she made were for the protection of her loved ones. Still, she was not as honest as my grandfather. I'm sure it was she who sorted through the box of photographs brought to me and my mother; she who removed Kjell's first wife from the family reunions, looking at each photo before she tucked them away somewhere. But upstairs, that afternoon, I found the one I was looking for, the one that slipped through because it was of thinner paper and had been cut with nail scissors into a heart shape. The wife was just the way I wanted her to be—thin and dark, a real sulky beauty—nothing like my mother.

Moggens didn't purposefully leave the "just married" photo of Kjell and his first wife out on his desk in the study. From the tarnish on the silver frame, I judged he'd never moved it since he set it there. Kjell's older face was more likeable, craggy and a bit ruined.

Back in the kitchen, my aunts clucked their tongues about Anders. It made Kjell fume. He told me that when they were children, he would row across the fjord while his sisters washed rocks with their tooth brushes. "Nothing is changed," he said.

My aunts told me that Anders used to have a meticulous and conscientious nature. They said that he was good with the children, that he could run a relay with an egg on a spoon clamped in his mouth, and never once lose the egg. They thought it was a shame what the change had brought: how he put his cigarettes out in his coffee cup, and used slang, and swore too much. "I want to piss," he'd say in the middle of dinner.

For two days, he'd complained of a crick in his back. My aunts humored him, and Lena told my grandfather to turn Anders's mattress, which he dutifully went and did. But in the kitchen Anders started up again.

"Damn," he stuttered, "damn," until finally my grandmother said to him:

"Damn crick in your back. That's right, Anders. Always something there is with you, always something there will be with you."

After she left the room, he made a fist and swung at the air, so sharply I heard his arm lock in the socket. Then he said very clearly to me, "There, the crick is gone."

"Someone is missing," my grandfather said as he took his place at the table laden with steaming crawfish and bottles of schnapps. "Ah, there she is, my wife." He made a toast and everyone looked around the table before they drank.

I'd been seated at the far end away from Anders, who stared glumly at his plate, which had been piled with food, precluding the interruption of his requests. I held Moggens's hand while he repeated a joke slowly for my benefit. His calluses felt like the ridges of a dried corn husk. I lost the gist of the joke. It seemed that I had been wandering around for days behind people, not knowing where I was going until we arrived, for days repeating words in Swedish after my grandmother—the words for electric stove, can opener, frying pan—none of them could I remember. I longed to lean my head against Moggens's chest so that I could hear the tones of his voice and cease to impute sense to the words. I didn't get the punchline of the joke, but when everyone laughed, I laughed too, laughed until my face felt like a mask I wanted to hold at arm's length and shake above the fire.

I left to have dessert with my seven tow-headed cousins at the children's table. They asked me to read the mustard and caviar tubes, and we all laughed at my pronunciation—laughed fit to kill. At least I knew what we were laughing about.

The sound of the sea moving back into a marsh is startlingly loud when you come upon it alone. I looked back towards the house and watched Anders slowly making his way to the center of the yard where the wreath of Midsummer still stood, dry and shaking apart in the wind. I thought of Marthe and how long it had been since anyone mentioned her name.

The children were flying past Anders's legs on an old sled that Kjell had fitted with wheels. They rode the sled in pairs. I reached the top of the hill in time to see another two launched. The boy steered while the girl lay beneath him and screamed.

The wind blew Anders's child-fine tuft of hair to the other side of his head, and he smashed it flat with the palm of his hand. Lena opened the back door and called him in. Ignoring her, Anders gripped the sides of his ambulator and whistled as the children went by. I waved to her and shouted that I would stay with him. Still, she called to him again. He turned and bellowed something ferocious, then, thrusting the ambulator ahead of him, he took a few more steps away from the house.

The long branches of the birch trees rose up in an arc and snapped back down with the force of the wind. The sky had grown heavy and thick with clouds. "*Vacket vader vi har iyen,*" I said, smiling at Anders. What weather we have. It was a phrase he had taught me the day before. He focused on that place in the air where he saw my face and began.

"I want … I want … I want to go …"

"Where?" I asked cheerfully, supplying him with, "to the sauna, to the boat, to the porch." But he didn't begin the teaching game, and the muscles of his face stiffened as he tried again.

Finally he managed: "I want … to go … fast."

"All right, Anders," I said. "All right, let's go fast for once."

I took the rope attached to the sled and moved a little farther up the hill. The children stood back in a semicircle, giggling at the prospect of their great-uncle and me on the sled. I lay down on it first and discovered that the handles also functioned as brakes, having a metal tab which could be brought to bear on the rubber tires.

Anders stood behind the sled and let himself fall forward. I was amazed at the strength of his arms as he caught and held himself above me. Then he covered me with his body, and I watched the tires sink into the ground.

He arched his back and removed my braid from under his chest. For a moment, he held it between thumb and forefinger, feeling the thickness of the plait, moving along it towards the nape of my neck. Then he tucked it gently under my chin, and placed his hands over mine on the controls.

Off we went, the grass occupying nearly the entire foreground of our view—a strip for water, a strip for sky. We hit a bump. The pier seemed to tilt upwards out of the water into the clouds. The boat's mast punctured the sky, and we came to a halt.

The children and I dragged the sled with Anders on it back up the hill. His cheeks were flushed, and the children had him laughing with their exaggeration of the strain. At the top, he refused to get off the sled, saying, "Myself ... this time alone."

The second time, he went down full speed. I watched him take the jolts of the uneven pier and soar off the end of it still holding onto the controls of the sled. I remember the moment fractured from time, hard as crystal, as though my own stillness could suspend him in the air, but I must have been running. After the splash, at the center of the widening circle of water, I saw Anders's pale hair spread like a dazzling quick bloom, then vanish. I dove for the glimmer of his white shirt and the flash of the sled's silver rail.

My fingers cramped with cold around a mug full of coffee and cognac, I told my new family that I had had Anders's hand in mine—that I'd let go when I could have saved him. The tears dripped from my grandmother's chin onto the table.

"No," Lena said, "he was seeking an oblivion. It was his will, not his weight ... those useless legs."

Then I remembered clearly and kept quiet. Anders had found my hand in the black water, though it was me that pulled away—for lack of air, yes, but mostly because of the shock of his firm grip. I had tried to shout my name into the water, swallowed the sound of it, and choked. I still don't know what made him realize I wasn't Marthe, his wife. But it was he who released me, not the other way around.

The plates in the kitchen were piled next to the sink, crawfish shells scattered along the counter. My grandfather paced between doorways, refilling his cup, leaving the kitchen, returning—stopping to run his hand over the back of my head. The room was humid from our tears and rank with the smell of fish. I got up to wash my face and came upon Kjell and my mother, standing in the foyer hugging.

I turned to walk into the other room, but Kjell had already seen me. He reached out with one arm and called my name, and I moved slowly into the center of their embrace. Before I closed my eyes and let my breath out against my mother's shoulder, I thought of Anders, swimming in the dark current where I hoped he'd find his wife.

Siobhan Dowd of International PEN's Writers-in-Prison Committee in London writes this column regularly, alerting readers to the plight of writers around the world who deserve our awareness and our writing action.

Writer Detained: Wang Dan
by Siobhan Dowd

*T*he Chinese Communist Party's ossified ideological tenets are like a double-edged sword. They help to maintain stability, but at the same time resemble a burning charcoal which cannot be cast from the hand."

So wrote Wang Dan, one of mainland China's most famous dissidents, in Hong Kong's *Ming Pao* newspaper. Wang has never been afraid to rebuke his country's leadership in the roundest terms. His brilliant and brusque essay style has found enthusiastic audiences both locally and abroad and has raised Wang from the volatile level of student leader (as he appeared on television screens around the world during 1989's ill-fated Tiananmen Square Democracy Movement) to that of an

Glimmer Train Stories, Issue 26, Spring 1998
©1997 Siobhan Dowd

uncompromising and acute intellectual. His credentials for a place in a future democratic government could one day prove impeccable, rendered the stronger by his current imprisonment on charges of conspiracy to subvert the government.

Wang Dan, twenty-eight, was a history student at Beijing University when, in the spring of 1989, the Democracy Movement unfurled. By the time of the movement's June 3 overthrow by the military, Wang had become one of its chief champions: a frequent leader of the rallies, a thin young man with thick-rimmed spectacles and a style neither flamboyant nor shrill, but rather staunch and grave. After the tanks rolled into Tiananmen Square, he was put promptly on the "most wanted" list. He handed himself in to the authorities and served three and a half years for counter-revolutionary incitement.

After being paroled in February 1993, he was told he could not re-enter Beijing University, so the next year he enrolled in a correspondence course in history at the University of California. He found himself living under close police surveillance: by the end of 1994, two unmarked cars were regularly to be found outside his family's apartment and police on motorcycles were following his every move. Nevertheless, Wang resumed his pro-democracy activities with undiminished determination. He wrote copiously for the domestic and international press and sent several petitions to the Chinese government on human-rights issues. One of his major themes was the pursuit of freedom. In one essay, entitled "Reflections on Freedom," it was Hegel, the German philosopher, not communism, that he blamed for much of the century's miseries. He wrote, "Hegel made a mockery of freedom when he claimed that 'freedom is understanding the inevitable.' ...It was precisely this that led Hegel to place the will of the state above that of the individual, a theory adopted by fascism ... But the pursuit of freedom has in fact always been at the centre of human society, a motivating force behind social progress and evolution."

In May 1995, Wang was one of the initiators of an open letter to the authorities marking Tiananmen Square's sixth anniversary, entitled "Draw Lessons from Blood." The petition was signed by eighty and pleaded with the government to rethink the events of 1989. The words fell on deaf ears. Wang was arrested two days after the petition became public and was held in incommunicado detention for seventeen months before being brought to trial in October 1996.

The prosecutors accused him specifically of contacts with hostile forces overseas and writing articles aimed at subverting the state. His parents were given only twenty-four hours to find a lawyer, and, in a trial that lasted three hours, he was found guilty and sentenced to a harsh eleven-year prison term. An official Chinese news agency claimed that, "Wang candidly confessed his activities; his criminality is clear, and the evidence conclusive." The presiding judge added, "Sufficient evidence, which included material, witness accounts, recorded tapes, and criminal technical appraisal"—whatever that may be—"were shown at court." Amnesty International, however, dismissed the proceedings as a "parody of justice." In an interview with the press afterwards, Wang's father commented that his son had admitted to writing articles, but had insisted that this was not tantamount to a crime.

His appeal against his sentence was dismissed the following month in a hearing that lasted only ten minutes. More recently, the Vice-Minister of Justice again rejected an application for parole filed by Wang's family, who report that Wang is suffering from a severe throat ailment and back pain. Readers are urged to add their weight to international efforts on his behalf by writing letters appealing for all charges against Wang Dan to be dropped.

Please send your letters to the following address:
His Excellency Premier Li Peng
Office of the Premier
Guowuyan
9 Xihuangcheggenbeijie
Beijingshi 100032
People's Republic of China

Chris Offutt

*Here I am at four years old in Kentucky. My mother
has few photographs of me as a child. This one is special
because "the picture man" came to the house with a camera
and pony. Many years later I worked as a child photographer
in the malls of New England. When I look at this picture
now, I marvel at a photographer with the courage to add a large
animal to the tricky mix of children, parents, and a camera.*

Chris Offutt is the author of *Kentucky Straight*, a collection of stories; *The Same
River Twice*, a memoir; and *The Good Brother*, a novel. He has traveled
throughout America and held over fifty part-time jobs. He is currently a
visiting writer at the University of Montana in Missoula, where he lives with
his wife and two sons.

CHRIS OFFUTT
Two-Eleven All Around

*W*hen she locked me out I didn't mind that much because things were drifty from the start. She didn't like my drinking and I did not go for her Prozac and police scanner. Her kid was a pain in the ass, too. As much as I tried to get along with him, he was already what he always would be—a sullen little punk who liked the couch.

What happened was I came home drunk and she wouldn't let me in. She didn't even answer the door. It was night and I thought I was doing good by coming home before the bars closed, but it didn't matter to her. I looked through the window and she was sitting hunched over her police scanner, not moving an inch. You'd think she was dead but I knew what was going on. She'd got on her high horse and was riding out a sober binge on anti-depressants. She did this the same way other folks went on Xanax and health food, sort of a home-grown detox. I could hear the static on her scanner, a steady sound like fast water until she squelched it and strangers spoke into the house.

At one time I tried to get into it, being a scanner head, thinking it was something we could share outside of drinking, fighting, and screwing. I even memorized part of the ten-code, what cops use on the radio. I never understood why they talk in code, though. A guide to it comes with the scanner, so it's not like they're fooling anybody. And saying ten-four instead of okay does not exactly save time in a crucial situation. My favorite was two-eleven all around, which meant that the subject was clean, with no warrants against him in the city or county. The lucky guy was free to go.

Nothing me and her did together was right except in the boinking department. It's not like she had a great body or nothing, just average, but it was attitude more than anything else. She'd do whatever came down the pike and not feel guilty later. Me, I'm all for weird sex, but sometimes thinking about it is better than the doing. Throw in a rope or a feather, and it's all she wrote for me. My best is in the afternoon, doing it regular while thinking about the weird stuff.

Funny thing about that scanner, though, it sucked her away from sex like getting religion. Where she used to kick up quite a ruckus, now she'd sit froze over that scanner for hours. She was patched into another world of good guys and bad guys, like a video game, except they were real. You'd hear the dispatcher call a cruiser with an address, and after a few minutes the cop says he's there. Then you sit and wait, tense and nervous, until the cop comes on the air with the subject's name, and checks for outstanding warrants. The weekends were the big nights, especially on a full moon. Just like us and sex in the old days.

Every few months, she'll go on Prozac, coffee, and the scanner, then get mad if I get hammered. It's not really fair but I understand she has to take time off from drinking, because when she's on safari, you better keep bail money handy. I could tell what she'd been up to the night before by the dents on the car. One thing, though, she didn't wake up with the regrets. She never called around to see if she did anything she should apologize for. To me, that made her a full-blown alcoholic while I was just a drunk.

The Prozac always made her lose weight. She looked great but couldn't have an orgasm. She said it was the Prozac that did it, but since she was on Prozac, she didn't mind. It bothered me a lot. I got to where I was so bad off I was jealous of that scanner. Jealous of men who would never touch her. Jealous of voices in the dark.

She never gave me a reason to feel that way, it's my trip, not hers, and it goes right to my father. He never drank a drop. He always held a job and lived in the same place all his life. What he did, though, was tomcat around with a different woman every day of the week. He made me cover for him when he slipped off to see his Tuesday girlfriend. Then on Wednesday he'd go bowling out of the county. Thursday he'd see a widow in town. He lived like a rabbit mostly, and you might say I had a few moms. These days I'm as loyal as bark to a tree.

Early on I asked her how many men she'd been with before me, and let me tell you, it's the stupidest damn thing you can ask a new girlfriend. I know that, but I did it anyway. I'm the kind of guy who'll do the stupidest damn thing at just the worst time. If a guy's got no nose, I'll tell him he's lucky his eyes are good, because he damn sure couldn't wear glasses. Sometimes I'm surprised I ain't got shot yet. I always figured that's how I'd go, killed at night by a stranger. Butte is that kind of town.

After I asked her how many men she'd slept with, she didn't say anything for a long while. There's a time period when you can tell that people are making up a lie, but hers stretched on so long, I knew the truth was on its way. Then it hit me that she was maybe counting up, and that number was something I did not want to hear. I wished I could shift to another channel. Just squelch her answer and move to someone else's life, let the cops and medics take over.

Finally she looked over at me and said, "What year?"

Well, that took the wind out of my sails, like getting kicked in the grazoint. And right there was where she was at—you ask a direct question and she'd answer with a question. She'd have made a great spy. She never gave a thing up. You could ask her if it was raining and she'd say, "Outside?" then not understand why I'd fly off the handle. We mainly lived at the top of our voices, even in the sackeroo. But I stuck by her. I might not be the biggest prize in the world, but I am not my dad.

The night she locked me out, I hid in the dark, watching her in the house. She's a big-boned woman who got pregnant young, quit school, and works as a waitress. Never got a nickel of child support. I guess you could say that breaks went against her, and getting mixed up with me might be one of those breaks.

Sometimes I watched her kid, which was easy because all he did was play video games. I couldn't get him to throw a baseball or football. When I was a kid my father didn't do anything with me, and now this boy wouldn't either. Sometimes I wondered if she was just using me to baby-sit, but I don't think so, no more than I used her place to sleep. Her kid wasn't that bad. He went to school, cooked for himself, and listened to his mother. He despised me and who could blame him. I was just another stranger roaming his house and sleeping with his mom. I was the enemy.

I stayed on the porch until I got sick of listening to the scanner's static and left. The house just sat there, dark and hard and locked. It was her house. Everything in it belonged to her, even her kid. My own boy was over a thousand miles away, back home in Kentucky. The way it works anymore is you don't raise your own kids. You raise someone else's while a stranger takes care of yours, and then when that doesn't work out, everyone moves along to the next person with a kid. It's like two assembly lines moving in opposite directions. At the end are grown kids who haven't been raised so much as jerked up.

You come to expect dealing with ex-husbands who don't like you, and kids who know full well you ain't their real daddy. And you know your kid's going through the same damn thing. Right now there's some somebody banging my ex and wishing my son was out of the picture. That's why I'm nice as pie to the kids of women I meet. It works out in the long run, and maybe someone'll be nice to my boy. He's fourteen and smart. He can be anything he wants to be.

The bars were closed and I walked an hour. I wasn't sober, but I wasn't completely drunk, which makes your mind go strange ways. I'm thirty-five years old and don't have a place to sleep, and right now I'm out of work. This is not what I had in mind when I left Kentucky. Sometimes I don't think I've done anything to leave my mark in this world. I guess I'm the kind of person the world leaves a mark on.

A patrol car cruised me but I stayed cool, and the cops probably made me for what I was—another poor bastard tossed out by his old lady. The second time they passed me, they didn't even slow down, and an idea hit me like a ton of bricks.

I cut down a few streets to an old industrial building that was getting renovated into an espresso joint. There was rubble lying in the street that looked like giant bread crumbs. I picked up a chunk and stood there a long time, thinking everything through, then I tossed it in a slow underhand arc through the plate-glass window. It made a beautiful sound that rang along the empty street like music. I leaned against a lightpole and waited. There was a grin on my face you couldn't wipe off with a chainsaw because I knew the police would come and ask for my ID. And I knew she'd hear it all. She'd hear the cop read my last name and ask for a ten-twenty-nine, which means check for wanteds. A minute would go by and the dispatcher would say, "Subject is two-eleven all around." And she damn sure knew the truth of that. I wasn't wanted anywhere, city or county, not even at home.

The cruiser came down the street, the candy rack on top flashing, no siren. I stepped away from the pole and held my arms away from my body, and the cop put a light on me like a poacher jacklighting a deer. There was no sound but my breath. The door opened and the cop came toward me, a black silhouette with his holster unsnapped, walking slowly in case I was hopped up on crank. I stood there waiting in that

J. LEON 97-

streetlight's glare with broken glass at my back and garbage at my feet and the whole galaxy over my head, and suddenly I knew damn sure what would happen one day.

I'll have my own place and a job. It'll be late at night and I'll be asleep. Someone starts banging at the door. I stagger over in my underwear and open the door and there's a stranger standing there, two or three strangers. Behind them in the street is an old shitbox out of Detroit, jacked up in the back. These punks are outside my door with patches of hair on their young faces, wearing boots and sleeveless shirts to show their tattoos. I stand there with my beer belly and think that even though I live alone in a little dump, dirty and cramped, it's still my damn place, and I'm willing to go down defending it. It's all I've got and it's not even really mine, just a rental, but I live here. You don't mess with a man in his own place.

I stand there in the night and look at these criminals, because that's what they are—there's nothing two-eleven about them. The street is empty and I'm alone. I don't want to show how twitchy I am on the inside and I say, "What the fuck do you want?"

And one looks at the rest with a sneer, and says, "See, I told you." Then he looks at me and says, "We're just hunting a place to flop, Dad."

It hits me who I'm looking at, a ripping that starts in my throat and runs to the soles of my feet. I can barely breathe. I hold onto the doorjamb to stay steady while I take a good look at this boy.

There's a part of me that wants to say, "Get a good look, son. Burn this in your brain, boy. See the grime along the molding? See the empty beer cans with cigarette ashes around the holes? See the beat-up furniture and the dirty sheets? Take a good look, son. Take a picture because this is where you'll wind up at, and you don't want it. You do not want this."

But I don't say it. I never gave him anything before. And now I can't even give him this.

Instead, I open the door wide.

NOMI EVE
Writer

Interview

by Linda Burmeister Davies

Nomi Eve's stories have been published in Glimmer Train, *the* Village Voice Literary Supplement, *and the* International Quarterly. *Eve earned her BA in English from Penn State University, and she has an MFA in fiction writing from Brown University. She has worked as a free-lance book reviewer for the* Village Voice, *the* Boston Globe, New York Newsday, *the* Jerusalem Post, *and* Publisher's Weekly. *She was recently awarded the Crossing Boundaries Award for Innovative Fiction by the* International Quarterly.

Nomi Eve

Photo credit Joanna Eldredge Morrissey

Eve is currently living in Boston with her fiancé, and continues to write the stories that are growing into The Double Tree, *a novel, which "will be done when it is done."*

Glimmer Train Stories, Issue 26, Spring 1998

You sent some great materials. One of the things that you said, that I don't think I've heard a writer say before even though I'm sure all writers think it, is, "I want readers to enjoy my work." Why do you suppose you would say it?

Well, writing is like a game of catch for me. I throw my words out and I want somebody to catch them. If I just throw them out and they go on forever, they're not doing their job. I spend the day writing and then Aleister, my partner, gets home and, I say, You have to listen to this. You have to listen to this. And I'll read him paragraphs or pages—it's funny—you haven't heard me read aloud, but for me, reading my work to somebody is as important as having them read it by themselves, because I know if it works. I can feel it. I can tell when I lose you in the middle of a sentence. That sort of magical communication that happens? It's like a different sense for me, like smelling or tasting. I can sense if I have you or not. And I need to know. If I just write it and nobody ever hears it, ever catches it, it doesn't work. And I'm a reader, too, and I love to enjoy stories. It's part of my work.

So you really are highly attuned to the reader.

Yes. This is something I learned after I graduated from writing school. After I finished Brown, I went to live with my cousins. I have these wonderful cousins in Philadelphia who saw me floating around and said, Oh, come live with us. So I went to live with them and I was writing and I didn't know who to read my work to. Suddenly I didn't have other writers around, and my cousin Joanie said, Well, read to me. She's a jeweler and an avid reader. So I started to read to Joanie and her daughter, Abby, who now is sixteen, and suddenly I realized that they were as good if not better readers than the writers in my graduate program, because they're just readers. They don't have their own voices in their heads, and from that moment on, and it's been five or six years now, I read to anybody I can get a hold of. My scientist fiancé, my artist mother, I mean everybody. It's just so important to me that they get it as well as that "the good writers" get it. And it's not one or the other. The things that really work are the things that really work for both of these camps.

Sometimes people think of literary fiction as having appeal really only for certain groups—well-trained intellectual ears.

And I want none of that. The people who aren't writers who read my work, I think, are responding to the same things that people who can talk about writing are responding to, but they're just readers. That was a big learning for me.

You'd probably be a great person to read your work for something like Symphony Space on public radio.

I'd love to do that. It would be a dream for me.

You should contact them sometime.

I still feel little. I know I'm getting there. I feel once my book is published … but now I still feel a little bit little. But it's exactly the sort of thing I want to do. Having this book published is a way for me to go around the country reading it. And not just ordinary readings, but real performances. I have to read you something. It has a music. It's so important for me to read.

What aspect of your writing has required the greatest conscious effort?

I've known for a while now that I've had a story to tell.

Since when?

Well, I'd say for the last four years. Four years I've been actively writing this book. And at the very beginning I wrote hundreds of pages, hundreds and hundreds of pages that no one will ever see. The story had such a complex timetable that I couldn't figure out how to do that. Where does the story start? That was the hardest thing. Where does this story start? Because it's not only my story, but it's a family story, and what does that mean? Does that mean it starts when the people in the family were born or does it start when I was told their story? Does it start with my birth? How much of it is my story? How much is it their story? Is it my father's story, because he told me part of the story? Or is it my grandparents' story because those were the people he was telling me about? So does it start with their birth? I was crazy over this. I remember I would write pages and pages and then I would make lists of the events and try to put them in an order. Nothing worked. I'm picturing myself sitting in my cousin's den making this list. And one day, once again, I was trying to write, trying to write, and I picked up one of my father's notebooks and copied a couple of sentences, and then I wrote the Esther and Yochanan story, and that was the start of it.

"Esther and Yochanan" was the start? Oh, I'm so pleased to hear that.

Yeah, you have it. Suddenly, I combined these times of telling. It was my "I write" and it was my father's "He writes," and it was the family story all at once. I wasn't conscious of this when I was doing it, but that's what happened and that changed everything.

Why was it so important to you, this consciousness of whose story it was?

Because I didn't know how to make visible what was going on inside of my head.

What I'm really curious about is why all that was going on.

Right. Why was that all going on. When I was twenty-one, my father told me a pretty shocking story, which I don't really want to go into right now, but it's really a pretty shocking family story that was horrifying and changed the way I—I mean everybody has their own family stories, and this was ours—which changed the way I thought about who I was and who my family is. It was a big shock for me. Suddenly everything I thought was true was different. Things made sense.

Isn't that something? Things make sense! And I thought I was insane.

Exactly! Things finally made sense. And other things made more sense: my father's writing of the family history, my grandmother's storytelling, all sorts of things suddenly had different meanings, and pretty intense meanings. Everything was connected. And for me as a writer, it was like walking into a book, like waking up and saying, Oh my God, my life is just like a book. It has all these images and stories and more images and more stories, and the reason I need to write this book is to try and explain that. To try and figure out my family history, which is a pretty major thing that we writers do, but it's what I need to do. I am compelled. And for me, that doesn't just mean to tell this story of what my father's told me, but to construct on paper this complex reality that I was born into. That's really what it's about. If I were to just tell you or tell anybody a certain family secret, that's not what it's about. It's about the communication, this triple-voiced communication. That's what it's about. It would be easy just to say, This is what he told me. But that's not what's so interesting about it. It's this very complex way we all have of communicating, and of telling our stories, and of not telling our stories that really fascinates me.

So that was a fantastically difficult, but positively life-changing conversation you had with your father.

Oh, yes. Thank goodness. Very difficult. Very positive. And I have only praise for the way my father's handled everything. We lead very difficult lives, and my father's coped in good ways and given me a tremendous gift. What a gift.

The gift of your own history is tremendous.

It took me a long time to realize that. He's been researching our family history since I was fifteen or so, even earlier, and he'd come down to dinner and say, Oh, we're related to this rabbi and that old rabbi. We didn't give him any peace. Oh, so what? So what? And he'd get these pictures sent from the royal portrait gallery in London, and we'd tell him to hang them up over the washing machine in the basement. We were merciless. And when I was in my twenties I started to realize this was a treasure.

It can be difficult to understand who we really are when we don't have the larger picture.

Well, I find that when we don't know the truth, we compensate by telling lots of other things in its place, and I know from my father's notebooks—and my grandmother is an amazing storyteller, and I think that both of those people are constantly trying to fill in things because the main story can't be told.

Should you have children at some future date, do you imagine being in your father's position of having a story you must tell them?

I had a pretty violent reaction to falsehood in my mid-twenties. I'm twenty-nine now. At around twenty-four, I became unable to lie. Even little things. I became very sensitive about little things and big things that have to do with truth. And I'm still like that, very very sensitive to truth. Funny, because I'm a fiction writer, but my fiction I think has a lot to do with truth. I blurt things out. I tell things. I can't help it. I say what I need to say.

That's a blessing, don't you think?

I find it a blessing in my life. But I don't have a choice. I really don't. That's just how I have to live my life. You need to give people information—you can tell the truth along the way. And you need to give them the tools to do the right thing with that information.

Did you anticipate being a writer as a kid?

Writers were always my heroes. They were always the most magical thing that one could be, and I read voraciously as a child, like a lot of writers do. I have memories of stacks of library books. And then when I got to college I went to my English advisor and said, I want to be a writer. He was a wonderful professor—Dr. Moore—and he said, Okay, sure.

He didn't make a big deal out of it. And then I found myself in all English classes. I didn't take writing classes. Something I really do not believe in is undergraduate writing majors. I think they should be abolished. I think they're hurtful. I think anybody who wants to be a writer should be a reader for a significant period of time, should be trained in reading, should be a good reader. When you're eighteen, you need to read. If you're gonna write you're gonna do it anyway, but you don't need to be in those writing workshops yet. If you want to do it, do it as an elective. I was a pretty hard-core English major with Shakespeare and all the things that we should read. I really believe that we need to read. And then when you're twenty-two, twenty-three—we're not talking about millions of years later—then do your writing school if you want to, if you need to, but I really don't think it's a positive thing for undergraduates. I believe that vehemently.

Does that mean you had bad experiences with it?

No. I avoided it. I didn't believe in it when I was eighteen. I was a literature major. I knew for me that I needed to be a literature major. I took elective writing classes.

The point then is to avoid getting shaped? Having your writing shaped, or what?

I think it's not so much avoiding the writing classes as it is gaining the literature classes, having that.

So reading is an essential base for writing?

Yes.

If you were to teach a creative-writing class, what would you try to communicate?

One of the things that I thought was missing in my own education as a master's student, was that nobody spoke to me about my writing in relation to my life, in relation to me, at all. It was your work and that's that. Let's talk about the work. There was no conversation about your relationship to your work in a real organic way. I have such a deep relationship to every word I write and to where this book fits into my life, that I think there should have been conversations about that. Writing is such a strange process. So strange. We never spoke about that. We never spoke about the process of a writer's life.

What do you mean by that?

Well, I was trying to write a certain chapter, a crucial chapter in my book, and I would spend the day writing and I'd think that I had done well, and then I would throw up. And Aleister would come home and he'd say, How was your day, Honey? and I'd say, I threw up again. I wrote a lot and I think it's good. And he'd say, It doesn't sound good. It doesn't sound like it should be this way. It had happened for a week. And then at the end of the week I started to read him what I had written, and it was awful. It was the wrong stuff. It wasn't right. It was covering up the truth. And my body was physically reacting to that. It was amazing. It was incredible and so strange, so weird. But that's what happened. I stopped writing that and I started writing the right stuff, and I stopped throwing up, just like that. And nobody in writing school tells you anything about that, and I'm sure it happens to other writers. It has to. But nobody says anything about that. About the different weird ways it fits into your life and your body. There are lots of things like that that I could have benefited from, I think, in a community of writers, having that sort of conversation. Besides studying books, wonderful books, and having people write, and getting critiqued, which I think is a wonderful situation to be in. I just think there's not enough talk—at least there wasn't in the program I was in—about writing and life, about how strange it is and how magical it is. Every single piece of my book has demanded something different of me, of my lifestyle, of my time commitment, every single piece.

Give me an example.

Well, now I'm at a point where I've been writing a little

amount of time a day, from half an hour to two or three hours, and producing tons of stuff, good stuff. Other times, I need a month to write a hundred pages no one will ever see. Of sitting there every hour of the day, doing it. And then the next month, I can write easily again. It just demands different time from me. Sometimes I'm incredibly productive in half an hour. Other times, I really need all day to get a paragraph.

Do you think that that is related to the material?

Very related to the material. Very related to the material.

So is it your experience that when you're on a road with material you want to be with, that you move more quickly?

Well, I think of my book as already existing. My book exists. It's sort of like the sculpture inside of a block of stone and I have to find it. My work is to find it. So when I'm close, it comes easier. When I'm far, it doesn't. As the writer of it, I have to find it. It's my responsibility.

When you feel something is your responsibility, what are you answering to?

It's my work in the world. It's why I'm here. Orthodox Jews wouldn't call me religious because I don't observe the Sabbath and I don't observe the Mitzvot, but I do have a pretty spiritual sense of my place in the world, within a Jewish context. And aside from answering to God, I just believe that I, Nomi, was set here in the world to do this specific work, and it's my responsibility and also my joy, but it's what I have to do, and that's to tell this story.

Now what's going to happen when you're done with this story?

I'm not a person who thinks, Oh, I have to write ten books, fifteen books. I might. I have to write this one. In the back of my mind, I have a thought that I need to write a book about literature. I'd love to write about other books. Maybe that will be my next calling.

I'd be terribly sorry if you stopped writing fiction.

Oh, I'll always be able to write fiction. But last month was the first time I was ever able to imagine a fiction beyond this one. It's been so all-consuming to me that I couldn't imagine. I have a framework that this book fits into, a context. A mission, so I can't picture the next mission. Most of my writing teachers never spoke to me about why they're doing what they're doing, their relationship to their work, their passion for it. Everything was much more focused on the individual work, on the piece, but it's about more than that.

In some of the psychology classes I've taken, I've noticed that people are sometimes so eager to make psychology look very scientific, very clean and predictable—as though that would dignify the field—that the soul of the thing is lost. Could there be something similar at work here?

That's where these things overlap. Psychology overlaps with literature. In soul. Conversations about the soul of a book, our own soul's relationship with a book. And that's where the magic lies. I think we're not yet ready, certainly not in academia, to have soul conversations.

Maybe we're afraid it will discredit us in some way. I just finished up an interesting class that looked at Multiple Personality Disorder. This particular instructor suggested that MPD is often inadvertently created by therapists—who expect to find it—when they try to isolate and exorcise non-integrated elements of a person's identity. One of the things we talked about is the fact that all of us have multiple voices, multiple identities. We are different people depending on the need of the moment, who we're with, all those things. Do you have ideas about why we are so concerned about being smoothly unified? You're obviously not committed to that idea at all.

Not at all. I—I've had my own dissociative experience. I guess I was twenty-three and I woke up one day in a crisis. I was going through a hard time psychologically, spiritually, and I woke up dissociative. There was another me in me. It was the most terrifying moment of my life. I was sure I was going crazy; I was sure I was sick; I was sure I was all those things the world says we are when we have such feelings.

And I had a wonderful therapist who said, No, you're not crazy. This is what happens sometimes. But that horror that I felt was hard to get over. Because even though I don't have those feelings anymore—that there's really another me in me, like I had felt—I've learned to feel that they're natural and normal and good, and if I need any proof of that I just look at my work and say, Oh, that's the Esther in me or that's the Gila in me or the Herschel in me. My friends know my characters and they say, Ooh, now you're being like so-and-so, and they recognize the different parts of me and the different people I make up.

I think it's a made-up fear—in response to your question—I think it's a story that as a society we've told ourselves. We think we should have just one self. I don't know why.

Well, thank God you had a good therapist! If you'd had someone busy trying to sort out and delineate separate identities and destroy the so-called alters, your life could be very different now.

My wonderful therapist said, Okay, who is it? Great! Love that part of you!

Much of your work is a mingling of connected voices. Was your development of this fairly unusual form connected to that dissociative time?

Very connected. It closely preceded it. I don't know if I would have been able to write what I'm writing if I hadn't had that experience, if I hadn't known that about myself. It opened me up.

You said that you showed some friends your writing and that they commented about the form being similar to the Talmud, and you said you were "stricken" by this comparison. What did you mean by that? Stricken as in you were struck by it or horrified by it?

Oh, in a good way. The history of that—you asked earlier what did I have to get over or deal with in order to start writing, and I said I had to figure out how to put on a page these three voices. Two voices, three. Every six months or so, I would get to a logjam in my work where I wouldn't been able to go forward, and the way each of these logjams has been reconciled is with the creation of a new form on the page. First it was the two voices, "Esther and Yochanan." The next was with the Sarah Aronson story which is called "Al Yud," which was in the *International Quarterly*, and that happened when I was at the MacDowell Colony. I had three voices I needed to put on a page, three things that I knew about this story that made this story real for me. It wasn't one of them, it was the combination of the three: the fiction and the history and my own Nomi voice reacting to it. No *one* voice told the story. And I wrote so many pages. Oh, my God. So many pages, trying to do this, until one day suddenly I put two columns on the page and just put it all there at once. This was revelation: Oh my God, there it is. Finally! And that was the second new form that solved this logjam. And when I showed those pages to a couple people who were with me at MacDowell, they said, Oh, that looks like a page of Talmud. And I said, Oh my God, you're right. After that, I consciously played with that and put one voice in the middle, and now I've been doing all sorts of things. And that really freed me up.

I completely forget where this question started. Oh. It began as a way to solve a problem. How do I represent the story as I know it? And then it ended up with an immense recognition: Yes, it's like a page of Talmud, and I understand why that makes sense both because I'm writing within a very Jewish context, and, practically, what is Talmud? It's an essential text and all these commentaries on it, and that's really what my work is about. It's playing with the notion of a central text, a central story. But the essential story, and the truth of it, or the reaction to it , or the way we live with it. It all made sense to me.

You spoke about that—having one text in the center and others at the edges, "undermining it, adorning it, chattering about it." What is the nature of the central text that places it in that position?

It's the story our parents tell us. It's our family history, the story we grew up with. The stories they tell us about ourselves and about themselves. And of course, whoever gives you your identity was also given their own. So it's a fluid thing, affected by what came before and by what comes after. So it's a parent's story, or grandparent's story, or great grandparent's story, and so on and so on. This has been made very visible and present in my life with my father's work. I've been given tons of these notebooks, my father's family-history notebooks, one after the other after the other. So for me, it's not just told, but it's been written down. Look at this—this is the very beginning. You'll recognize that. This is the essential story, which doesn't necessarily mean it's true. It just means that that's what's given to you. The one in your hand is the least detailed of them. This is what my father wrote after his father died, specifically my grandfather, whose name was Peretz.

Oh, yes, the one who lived. [From her story "To Conjure the Twin."]

This is one notebook. My father has taken the four grandparents and given each of them a book, longer than this and more detailed. So in my work, I use this as my essential story, and then fill in from the other notebooks.

So he is as driven—

Oh, he's more driven than I am.

What is this? Is it that secret thing?

I think so, but we're compulsive people. That's got to be part of it. We have a job that we need to do. We just need to do this.

I noticed in the book review you wrote that you are very generous. I don't mean that you're being lax, or less than truthful.

I only review books that I really love. There will not be one negative review that comes out of my pen. I don't think that's my work. Let somebody else do that. I won't say a word about a book I don't love; I won't review it. I'll only review books that I love.

Why is that?

It's just who I am. It's what I can do. I'm sort of lucky as a writer. A lot of writers have mediocre work published. My writing is either really good or really bad and it's recognizable as either, and if I try and write something that's not me, that's not a love story, then it falls into the category of bad, and it never reaches the light of day. It's very cut and dried for me. Which is a blessing, but makes my work hard along the way. Some people will have their books published before mine, they'll have more stories published than I will, all of those things, but in the long run, I know it's a blessing. But it's strange.

You mentioned that you identify with George Eliot. Why?

I just love her writing. She writes a lot about soul. She actually uses the word soul a lot. And she tells great stories. I don't know if it's so much that I identify with her as that I love reading those books. And also the vocabulary is wonderful. Big vocabulary. Meaty. If I compare her with Jane Austen, well, for me, there's no comparison. I like Jane Austen, but it's almost like a skeleton compared to what George Eliot does. George Eliot talks about the science of soul and the religion of body.

Where was your first story published?

The *Village Voice Literary Supplement.* I was an intern there which meant that I opened mail, and I was lucky enough that the editor, a woman named M. Mark, looked at me from the get-go and said, You can do, can't you? She didn't treat me like an intern; she treated me like a writer. She let me write book reviews right off the bat, and then when I was there four months, she said, Well, let me see a story. At that point, I was in my difficult time and I hadn't written in over a year. This was a Friday afternoon. And I went home. This was such a crazy time in my life. I wasn't earning any money as an intern, so I would spend five days a week in New York sleeping on friends' couches, and then I'd go home on the weekends to my cousins' in Elkins Park, Pennsylvania. So it's a Friday afternoon and she says, I want a story from you, and I hadn't written in around a year, and I went home to my cousins' house, and that weekend I wrote the "Double Tree" story at their living-room table, and read it to my cousins Joanie and Abby. They sat on either side of me and I read it to them and we just knew. Here it was. I could do it. And I brought it in to M. on Monday, and Tuesday she said, Of course. I walked around New York City with a smile on my face. It's a special smile I get. I've been lucky to have it five times now when my work has gotten out into the world.

How old were you then?

Twenty-three, twenty-four.

When you say that you believe this is your mission, I guess, as intense and difficult as those years were, you were lucky not to have had to wander around missionless for decades like most of us do.

I feel very lucky. Because I had those years, and I always believed I would get out of them, and I had work to do. But in order to do my work, I felt that I had to fight against the messages that the literary establishment was sending me, as a young writer. It seems that the literary world wants young writers to churn out stories. First, a collection, and then a novel, and then another novel. There is a path laid out for young writers, but I don't think it's necessarily a natural path for everybody. For a while I was trying to fit into it myself, trying to write these discrete, self-contained stories, and I realized I don't fit into that at all. I don't see this first work as my early work. I see it as my life's work. When I got to MacDowell, which was a wonderful place for me, I told people—and this was only a year and a half ago—I told people that I needed ten more years to write this book, and I'd already been writing for four years. A few months ago, I spoke to a painter from MacDowell, Mark Wethli, a wonderful painter, and he said, So, Nomi, how's the writing going? And I said, Two, three more years, and he said, Nomi, you've made great strides! At McDowell, you said a decade. But the time doesn't matter. Whatever it takes.

What do you do when you're not writing? How do you make a living? People think they're going to support themselves with their writing and that's very difficult. There aren't enough readers.

Well, I've had crazy years. They're getting less crazy. But for two years, I wrote a lot of book reviews and made a good amount of money—not enough to support an apartment in New York, but a good amount. Then I stopped book reviews and I went to Israel, and I didn't do anything but write for a while. I had saved a little bit of money and my grandmother gave me a little money, and I just sat and wrote. For the last six months or so I've been back in the States, living in Boston with my wonderful fiancé, Aleister, a scientist, a post doc at Harvard. And I recently got a job teaching English as a second language, and that's what I do in the morning from 9:00 to 12:30, and then I write. I've also taught Hebrew school. Every season is different. I never make a ton of money, but the past month I made as much as my scientist sweetheart teaching various things.

I think this English-as-a-second-language thing is going to be good for me. I enjoy the teaching, and schedule-wise it's terrific. I can tell them month by month if I want to work because the courses are a month long and they pay pretty decently. I wouldn't be able to have kids and support a family on what I make right now, but we're doing okay. We're not saving anything, but we're doing okay. And various people have been generous in my life. It helps a lot. I'm so lucky. I have such a supportive family. When I said I was taking this English-as-a-second-language job, both my parents asked, Is this going to give you time to write?

You know the idea of the central text and the things around it—I'd like to see you draw a picture of you either in words or with lines.

Let me hold the pen and paper in my hands. You know, I think it's too off the wall for me. Not off-the-wall crazy, but I'm horrible with a pen in my hand. I'm only comfortable at a typewriter. I don't know what it is. When I was in high school, I wore a hand brace for a while because of bad joint pain. Now I can barely read my own handwriting. The portable computer was revelatory for me, being able to take it with me. So I would just say that if I had to draw a picture of myself, it would be this page or the next page [from one of her stories], the I, Nomi, voice. This is fiction that I'm actually having one of my characters write. And this is fiction, too, but it's *my* fiction.

So in terms of what I look like on the page, when I look at one of these pages, I recognize myself in a big way. Here, I like this one. Here I have my Nomi voice, who I am. This is my father's voice, who he is. And this is fiction, one of my character's writing. So here are actually three generations writing at once. Want me to read a little?

Sure.

I'll read you from here to there.

Avichail is the name of my grandparents' village and it's where I grew up spending summers and where, besides Jerusalem, a lot of my stories take place. It's a *moshav* outside of the city of Natanya.

> Avichail is a small beautiful place. When I walk there I feel like I am walking in the palm of my family's hand.
> The flower-lined roads are skinlines—our fortune written in the ficus trees, in the water tower cascading with purple bougainvillea flowers, written in the triangular concrete bomb shelter jutting out of the earth.

Like so many writers-in-waiting, as a child I read voraciously. Books with their portable bodies and borders are my third home country. The country that I can take with me whenever I cross the ocean. The country that exists, according to my whim and taste, within the small territory of my own hands.

But it was not only the fact that I could take them with me that made books essential. I think I read so much as a child in order to prepare myself to read my life. All of this writing is really an act of reading. I am fully involved in making visible the tale that I was born into.

I grew up speaking three languages: English, Hebrew, and the Language of Books. Languages consist of grammar and vocabulary—skeleton and skin. The Language of Books is skeletoned by story and is fleshed out by characters, metaphors, so many words giving face to meaning. And in this sort of speech, our family was over-eloquent. We have so many symbols, so much drama, tension, tragedy, both obvious and hidden. I wonder if there wasn't someone crafty, more than a bit cruel, hunched over the desk in the little room downstairs, writing our lives in the seconds before we lived them. And yet, I always thought those were our words we were speaking.

That was as good as any picture.
Both my mother and my aunt are visual artists. Our house is filled with art, and I have an incredible absence of talent in that realm. I can't draw. I knew early on that this was not for me.

As complex as truth is, with all the sides there are to see it from, what can we be sure of in the world?
I believe in truth. I believe in truth as a sort of force in

the world like color. I believe that truth exists like the sun shines in the sky, and that we're in relationship to it, and what we can hang onto is that relationship. We can work on that relationship. Because of who I am, my work involves being very sensitive to that. So I guess I'm answering in two ways. One, that I very much believe in truth as an actual force. It's not just a word. And in terms of what we hang onto, I believe in that existence of truth, and I believe in my own life's work—I need to write this book, and have a family, and love the people around me.

One of the pieces that you provided about the very old rabbi and the very young wife, my initial response to that was to be, not offended, but to have, still, an aversive reaction. But before you were done, I realized I had to let go of that.

That story has a funny history. I was given that story years ago. It's a true story, this murder, and there's a lot more of it that never got put into it because there was so much history that I had to deal with. There were pages and pages and pages and pages. I had a lot of trouble weeding it out and focusing on just a bit of it. Another trouble I had was that I only write love stories.

And here was a murder story.

Yes! So what do I do? I cannot write the murder. I tried for years to write that story, and then around a year and a half ago, came this one paragraph—the first paragraph about old Herschell pondering soul. He was such a nut, but I really loved him, and his thoughts are really my thoughts, and I love that, too. Everything he thinks, I've thought, and he became the home for those thoughts, and then suddenly he loved Chasia and I believed in his love for her. And you know what? I've spoken out of both sides of my mouth. I have a cousin in his forties or so, and he's dating a much younger woman, and I tell him to keep away from her: It's not right—go away from her. And meanwhile, the same evening I was telling him this, he

was there when I read this Herschell story. But as much as I
believe in Herschell's love for her, I also have these other
feelings.

But they love each other so much, they do. You know, I'm
not finished with her. Chasia has been in my head so long, and
I've been loving this young Chasia woman even though she's
not directly in my lineage—I just have loved her so much, and
I felt, okay, I'm done with this Herschell piece, but I'm not
done with Chasia. And she's come back in this funny piece
where I have the twins ["To Conjure the Twin"], when they
are children, go once a year to visit their grandfather, who's
Esther and Yochanan's son—he'd be my great-great-great or
something like that. And his name is Yehoshua, and in his real
life they did go once a year to visit him, and they would run
around the walls of the city—this was their big memory of the
visit. And so I have this Yehoshua character obsessed with the
story of the murder, and he tells the grandchildren every year
when they come back: The story happened right here in this
house. And they fall in love with this Chasia woman, these
adolescent boys. So she comes back in their dreams. I think I
have this story with me. I must read you one more thing, from
here to there. He is Yehoshua Shine, the twins' grandfather
and Esther and Yochanan's son. He lives in the same house in
Jerusalem where everybody else lived.

> Yehoshua Shine was unable to sleep. Night was a
> wide place holding him prisoner. And he could not,
> either with potion or prayer, manage to find the key.
> He would settle into bed, turn over the pillow so that
> it was cool, and then shut his eyes. But always, instead
> of sleep, he would see the entire story condensed into
> a single repeating image. The image was of the young
> Widow Herschell, his step-grandmother, sitting in an
> open carriage in front of the house on Rev Pinchas

Street. The Widow Herschell, a woman he had never met. Young when married. Young when widowed. His mother had once told him, "Beauty like a vine, hers was; it climbed all over you, made you feel covered with precious flowers." "Flowers." Yehoshua mouthed the word as he sat up in bed. Chasia was sitting in the carriage looking towards the house. Recently widowed, she was leaving Jerusalem for Sephat. It was a stagnant image. The horses were the only part of the picture displaying kinship to motion, their front hooves were in the air. "Sephat," Yehoshua whispered, "where prayers float amongst the houses like gentle clouds, but not obscurant at all." The words were those of a famous contemporary mystic. Yehoshua smiled. He was proud that despite his exhaustion, he had remembered them.

Such was the nature of Yehoshua Shine's insomnia. There was an image embedded in the sleep loam of his soul. And he could not dislodge it. He had been trying for several weeks. The nights were all the same. He would lie awake, not wrestling with the image, but receiving it. It was, he knew, some sort of foreign correspondence, a message sent his way from far away. "Only," he groaned, "it has gotten stuck in the conscious cogs of my inner machinery." He groaned again and turned onto his side, and then onto his other side. But he could not sleep, no matter the position. He was so uncomfortable. The night ticked away.

Some time later, Yehoshua decided to examine the image more closely, so he closed his eyes and peeked into the carriage. Chasia's child was lying next to her, a baby in a traveling basket, covered with blankets. The baby, he knew, was doomed. It would die several months after Chasia's departure, of scarlet fever. Yehoshua puckered his lips and leaned towards the infant in his mind. He was very confused. But he kissed the air anyway. And somewhere in the night of this city or that one, a child cooed. After her baby died, Chasia married a successful dye merchant. Whenever Yehoshua imagined Chasia's dye merchant, he pictured a slight man with dark eyes whose fingers were stained, each a different color. Yehoshua breathed deeply.

On a whim, he got out of bed and pressed a hand to his ear, and jumped up and down on one foot, and then the other. But the image would not come out. He shook his head so hard that the room began to spin and he felt nausea in his face and belly. When he lay back down again, shaking, he was embarrassed by his mechanical attempt at dislodging the disturbance. "But," he reasoned, "I cannot be blamed for trying." He finally fell asleep somewhere just before dawn.

Several hours later, a very tired Yehoshua Shine rose from bed, and went to his window and looked down to Rev Pinchas Street, but he did not see the carriage there. "No," he mused, "it is in my head, only." Shuffling over to the wash basin, he dipped his hands in the cold water and splashed his face. Then he turned towards the window with his face still dripping and asked the emptiness, "What am I, my Lord? A quarry for your sighs?" For several moments he stood there, feeling the image embedded like a family fossil, a petrified piece of the past that had gotten lodged in him. "Indeed," he thought, "flowers." Yehoshua reached for a towel and patted his face with it. Then he began to say his morning prayers.

So Chasia did have a baby, they did have a baby. It's not in that other piece. But the baby did die. That's my work in progress. That's new. I have had this picture in my head for three years now, this picture of Chasia just sitting in that carriage. This one image. That's what I write from. I write from these single images that get stuck in my head.

Peter Lefcourt

J'Accuse! *Even at the age of five, I was possessed with an acute sense of social justice. When two members of Bunk 12 at Camp High Point were disciplined for participating in a Jell-O fight, I ferreted out those actually responsible for the errant splatterings of Jell-O and brought them to justice.*

Peter Lefcourt has published four novels—*The Deal, The Dreyfus Affair, Di and I,* and *Abbreviating Ernie*—appreciated by a small but loving readership. In reviewing his latest novel, Kirkus wrote, "Lefcourt sinks to new lows ... ," a judgment he is very proud of, considering the source. His day job is screenwriting, where he toils in the absurd demimonde of Hollywood. He is the only screenwriter in history to have kept Joan Collins in the same wardrobe for thirty-five pages.

PETER LEFCOURT

Closure

*E*very Wednesday during the season I drove Edgar
Dent out to Santa Anita. He liked to have a bowl of chili in the
Clubhouse Grill, then sit in the infield and bake his face in the
winter sun. He bet chalk for nine races and went home, a
hundred bucks up or down. You would have thought that at
his age he'd try a few longshots, but Edgar said you didn't get
to be eighty-six by taking flyers. At this point, he maintained,
he was playing with house money.

I had met him three years ago when he collapsed standing
next to me at the rail at Hollywood Park. I helped him up and
asked if he wanted medical attention. He just blew his nose and
squinted at the board to see if the photo finish was official.
Then he asked me if I were going anywhere near Hollywood
after the ninth race.

So I gave him a lift home, during which he didn't say a whole
lot. When he talked at all, he talked about the horses. Just
before he got out of the car, he said, "You going out next
Wednesday?"

"Probably."

"Stop by here at a quarter to. The goddamn bus takes
forever."

Since that day I drove him to the track pretty much every

Wednesday except in the summer, when the horses were in Del Mar. He lived in a sagging bungalow in Hollywood, next to a Three-Day Tire store. He had no phone, no refrigerator, and a thirteen-inch black-and-white TV with tinfoil on the antenna. I figured that anybody who didn't have a phone wasn't exactly rolling in it.

On the few occasions that I tried to learn something more about him he made it perfectly clear that it was none of my business. And that was that. You didn't pursue conversations with Edgar Dent that he was not inclined to have.

The only exception Edgar made to betting favorites was an occasional mudder. He liked to put twenty on the nose of a horse that looked good on a sloppy track. They never came in. Except once—on a rainy day last February when Edgar took the entire trifecta purse of the fourth race at Santa Anita. He had bet three longshot mudders, two at ninety to one and the other at sixty to one. They finished one-two-three, in the order that Edgar had bet them, paying $10,986. That was on a two-dollar bet. Edgar had put twenty down.

"Jesus," I said, "that's over a hundred grand."

Edgar just shook his head and muttered, "You see that two horse come out of nowhere?"

At the payoff window Edgar was given a form to fill out with his name, address, social-security number, and a 1099 form reporting his earnings to the government.

"Are you yanking my chain?" he protested to the clerk, who told him that all winnings over one thousand dollars had to be reported to the IRS.

"Sorry, that's the law."

Edgar stared at the form for a while, frowned. "I don't have a social-security number."

Edgar might as well have said he didn't have an esophagus.

"You don't have a social-security number?"

"That's what I just said."

66

The clerk told Edgar that in the absence of a social-security number, they would have to withhold the maximum amount—39.6 federal, 9.3 state.

Edgar did the math and growled, "That's 48.9 %. You going to take half my winnings?"

"That's the law."

Things got worse when the clerk told him that he couldn't be paid in cash. That, too, was the law.

"You mean to tell me you don't have fifty grand lying around here?"

"All payoffs of over ten thousand dollars are made by check."

They issued Edgar a check for $54,397.59. We were halfway home when Edgar asked me where my bank was.

"Sunset and Doheny."

"You mind going in there and cash this?"

"They won't do it."

"They don't think Santa Anita's good for fifty-four grand?"

"They have to put a hold on funds against deposits, and I don't have fifty-four thousand dollars in the bank. Nowhere near that. Why don't you open your own bank account? In Hollywood. Near your house."

"I don't like banks."

"You're not going to keep fifty-four thousand dollars around in cash, are you?"

He didn't reply. We drove in silence for a while, then he said, "What if I signed it over to you and you put it in your bank account and then gave me the cash after they put the hold on it?"

"You want to trust me with fifty-four thousand dollars?"

"Why not?"

"You don't even know where I live. I could just disappear, and you'd never see the money again."

"You planning on doing that?"

"No."

"So what's the problem?"

The teller at my bank looked at me strangely as she examined the second-party check from Santa Anita. She, too, had to go confer with her supervisor, who came out and asked me if Mr. Dent had a local bank reference.

"Why would you need that?"

"We have to report all deposits of more than ten thousand dollars to the government. There are tax ramifications."

"Oh, you don't have to worry about that. The IRS already took their cut off the top at the race track. Nobody's stiffing the government, trust me."

The supervisor said the hold would be ten days. I pointed to the sign that said the hold was seventy-two hours. He pointed to the fine print in a deposit agreement that he removed from a drawer that you couldn't have read with an electron microscope.

"How about we compromise? Seven days?"

Check in hand, he went back behind closed doors to confer, presumably, with his supervisor. When he emerged he said, "The best we can do is next Wednesday morning, after ten."

I showed up at 11:05 A.M. the following Wednesday with a Lufthansa airline bag. The supervisor and I counted out the money together at a table in front of the safe deposit vault. Fifty-four stacks of ten one-hundred-dollar bills. I walked out to the lot with my fifty-four thousand dollars and drove to Edgar's house in Hollywood.

"You're early," he said.

I handed him the Lufthansa bag. "I thought you'd want to put this in a safe place. Like in the bank."

He looked at the money, then stuck the bag in a closet which contained what looked like several disassembled vacuum cleaners and walked out the door.

"You got any plans for the money?" I asked him after he got in the car. Instead of replying, he took out the form and started doping the double. And that was that.

He lost all nine races that Wednesday and was in a foul mood all the way home. He passed up the post mortem and stared gloomily out the window. When I pulled up in front of the house, he asked me to wait for a moment. He went in and returned with the airline bag.

"You want to give this to Frances Bidden?"

"Who?"

"Frances Bidden."

"Who's Frances Bidden?"

"It doesn't matter. Just give it to her."

"Where do I find her?"

"Santa Monica. She's in the book."

"You want me to find an address in the phone book, go there, and hand this person fifty-four thousand dollars?"

"Yeah."

"Do you want me to tell her who it's from?"

"She'll know."

"Look, Edgar, this sounds like a personal thing. Maybe you should do this yourself."

"Take a grand off the top for your trouble. Just do it. Okay?"

I stood there holding the satchel of money, trying to figure out how to get out of this. But Edgar wasn't taking no for an answer.

"You mind going now? 'Baywatch' is on."

So I left. Once again with fifty-four thousand dollars of Edgar's money in my possession. And instructions to deliver it to a woman named Frances Bidden in Santa Monica.

I slept poorly that night, as a heavy rain bounced off the roof. I woke up groggy and stiff. After two cups of coffee, I considered my options. I could go cash my disability check. Don't ask. I could go out to Santa Anita and reinvest Edgar's money in another couple of mudders. Or I could drive to Santa Monica and give Frances Bidden fifty-four thousand dollars and be done with it.

The West Side and Santa Monica phone book had an F. Bidden on Navy. It would take me twenty minutes. I got in the car and headed south on La Cienega, west on Pico.

The address on Navy Street was a faded blue stucco bungalow, with a couple of desiccated orange trees on what passed for a lawn. I sat parked across the street with my Lufthansa bag full of money, staring out into the rain and wondering what the hell I was going to say. Hello, my name is Michael J. Anthony ...

Eventually I got out of the car and went across the street and up a walk littered with dead palm fronds and eucalyptus nuts.

I knocked several times before the curtain on the sunporch parted. It was hard to see clearly through the smudged window. There was a face. With a cigarette in the mouth.

I waved. Then pointed at the airline bag. As if that explained everything. She didn't open the door. I shouted through the glass and over the noise of the rain, "I've got something for you." And I pointed again to the bag.

An old Labrador stood behind her barking perfunctorily. Finally, she opened the door a crack.

"Are you Frances Bidden?"

She looked at me closely. That's when I saw her eyes for the first time. In the middle of a face dry and wrinkled with age were a pair of liquid and compelling eyes.

It was approximately at that point that something registered in that soft vulnerable core inside all men that renders us helpless at moments when we need to be anything but. I felt for Edgar. Though I had no idea why.

It took me a moment to recover. Meanwhile, the Labrador stopped barking and retreated into the house. I said to Frances Bidden, "I have something for you."

When she still didn't say anything, I went on.

"It's money. Edgar Dent asked me to give it to you."

At the mention of Edgar's name, her features tightened. And

she spoke for the first time. It was barely above a whisper. "Who was that?"

"Edgar. Edgar Dent."

"I wouldn't take a nickel from that son of a bitch," she said, articulating the words carefully to make sure I understood, before closing the door to the sunporch, entering the house, and locking the door behind her.

As I drove to Hollywood, I wondered what the hell Edgar had done to this woman to make her so angry. And when. The woman was eighty if she was a day. Whatever it was it looked as if she had been carrying it around with her for a long time.

Edgar wasn't thrilled to see me.

"It's Thursday. What are you doing here?" Then he saw the Lufthansa bag and said, "I thought you were going to give her the money."

"She wouldn't take it."

I tried to hand him the satchel, but he just stood there and glared at me.

"Look, I don't know what you did to this woman, but she thinks you're a son of a bitch."

"What I did to her? You don't want to know what she did to me?"

"No, I don't."

"She drove me crazy. Day in and day out. For five years. She drove me crazy. Out of my head."

"So why do you want to give her fifty-four thousand dollars?"

"She wanted a De Soto. Badgered me for a De Soto. For years. That's all I heard about. They don't make De Sotos anymore, so I figured I'd get her a Cadillac. She can't complain about a Cadillac. That's about what they cost these days. Loaded. I checked with the dealer."

I took a deep breath and put the satchel down at his feet and said, "Take the fifty-four thousand dollars, go to a Cadillac dealer, buy a car, register it in her name, and have them deliver it to her."

"I don't know what color she wants."

"What difference does it make?"

"I don't want any more bitching."

"Then break in there and force her to take it. You know, tie her up and leave the money at her feet."

"You got to do this for me."

"Sorry. I quit."

And I turned around and walked back to my car, leaving the airline bag at his feet. I got in and, just before I started the motor, looked back. He had closed the door and left the bag outside.

I got as far as La Brea before I did a U-turn and drove back to Edgar's house. The bag was still lying there at his door getting rained on.

I drove back to Navy Street speeding, running a light at Venice and nearly broadsiding a Volvo with a car seat in it. I decided that the simplest thing would be to leave the bag on the sunporch and walk away.

But just as I got there, the door to the sunporch opened, and she emerged in a raincoat, with an umbrella and the Labrador on a leash. I watched her turn up the street, moving with surprisingly erect posture for a woman of her age.

Grabbing the satchel, I got out of the car, hurried across the street and up the walk.

As soon as I opened the door to the sunporch I heard the sound of the tumblers turn on the door that led to the house. I looked up and saw another old woman standing in the doorway and holding a gun in an unsteady hand.

"Don't move a goddamn inch," she said.

It took the Santa Monica police about ten minutes to get there. As the old woman held the gun with one hand and a cell phone with the other, I tried to explain to her the purpose of my being on her sunporch, but she didn't lower the gun.

Sergeants Trujillo and Hofgren got out of the squad car and approached the house. When they saw the old woman with the gun, they ordered her to lay the gun down on the floor. While one of them held his weapon on me, the other frisked me, turned me around, put my arms in back, and cuffed me.

Hofgren asked the old woman what happened. She said that she had caught me breaking into the house.

"I wasn't breaking into the house. I was just trying to leave something."

"What?" asked Trujillo.

"There's an airline bag on the sunporch with money in it. I wanted to give it to Frances Bidden."

"Who's Frances Bidden?" Hofgren asked.

"My sister," the old woman answered. "She's walking the dog."

Trujillo went and got the Lufthansa bag. He opened it, saw the rolls of hundred-dollar bills, and showed it to his partner.

Hofgren asked the old woman, whose name was Eunice, if the money was hers. She shook her head. Then he asked her if I had taken anything from the house. Eunice shook her head again.

Then he asked me if this was my money.

"It's Edgar's," I explained.

"Who's Edgar?"

"He lives in Hollywood. He asked me to give this money to Frances Bidden."

"Frances don't want any money from him," Eunice said.

Trujillo and Hofgren seemed unsure how to proceed.

Leaving me standing there handcuffed on the front walk, the two cops walked back to the car to confer.

"So you know Edgar?" I asked her while the cops were talking.

"I never had the goddamn pleasure. And just as soon never

would."

"You must have heard about him?"

"Nothing good. Believe me."

The cops returned, told Eunice they'd be in touch, and put me in the squad car. When I tried to explain things, they told me that I had the right to remain silent.

At the station house, they asked me if I wanted to call a lawyer. The only lawyer I knew I owed money to. Don't ask. So I sat there in a cubicle while Hofgren ran my name, looking for a rap sheet, and Trujillo called my bank at Sunset and Doheny to corroborate my story that I had cashed a check for fifty-four thousand dollars there.

The bank checked out. But the computer in Sacramento spit out $670 of unpaid parking violations. They called Los Angeles to ask if they should hold me for pickup on an outstanding warrant. Los Angeles didn't have the manpower available at the moment, so Santa Monica had either to book me on the breaking and entering or let me go.

Trujillo took me into the interrogation room, removed the handcuffs, sat me down, offered me a cup of coffee, and asked, "You want to run this whole thing by me?"

I told him the story, starting with meeting Edgar at Santa Anita, right through to the Cadillac. When I was finished, he shook his head and whistled, "The trifecta paid ten grand?"

"Yeah. Three longshots. Two of them went off at ninety to one."

"No shit."

Hofgren returned and told Trujillo that Eunice just said on the phone that the door to the sunporch had not been locked. Technically, therefore, I was not breaking and entering. I was only trespassing.

They talked about this for awhile. Trujillo told Hofgren about the trifecta.

"Ten grand. Jesus."

So they told me to take the money back to Edgar and forget about it. Hofgren called me a cab from his desk. When the cab arrived I said good-bye to them, took my bag of money, and walked out of the police station.

The cab dropped me on the corner of 19th and Navy. As I was unlocking my car door, I heard a cracked whistling sound from across the street. Frances Bidden was standing in the doorway beckoning to me.

I walked across the street and up the walk. Frances stood in the open doorway to the sunporch and told me that I'd best not have anything to do with Edgar Dent.

"Believe me, I know what I'm talking about," she said.

"Look, I'm just supposed to give you the money."

"He don't give you anything for nothing. There's always a price."

Eunice appeared in the open doorway. "Tell him about the parakeet," she suggested. Frances Bidden's eyes lit up at the memory.

"Edgar brings home a parakeet one day. To the house in Culver City. This parakeet wasn't right from day one. Never sang a note. There was something wrong with the parakeet, but I didn't find out till later that Edgar had gotten him secondhand from his brother-in-law. He had told me it cost twelve dollars in the pet store."

"That's terrible," I said.

"Never sang a note."

"Twelve dollars."

"That was in 1937. Twelve dollars meant something."

"Well, he wants to give you your twelve dollars back." I pointed to the bag in my hand.

"The parakeet's nothing. What about the De Soto?"

"The De Soto was the last straw."

"With a pearl-handled steering wheel and white walls," Eunice elaborated.

"He promised me a De Soto. With one of them pearl-handled steering wheels, you know? And white-wall tires. He even showed it to me at the car dealer. Over on Ocean."

We were standing there at the door of the sunporch. Though it had stopped raining, I was tired and hungry. I hadn't eaten anything since breakfast. I didn't want to hear about the De Soto.

So I merely put the satchel down at her feet, smiled, and said, "I think that's terrible. Anyway, here's money for a new De Soto."

"They don't make De Sotos anymore," she said.

"Buy a Cadillac. They're even better. I got to go."

That's when Eunice pulled the gun out of her cardigan again. "Take that goddamn money with you."

I took the airline bag, and, as I started to walk away, I heard Eunice say, "A Cadillac ain't a De Soto."

I put the money in the trunk of my car and drove away. All week long I tried to convince myself to take the money, buy myself a Cadillac, piss it away, give it to charity, anything. Just get rid of it.

The following Wednesday I showed up at Edgar's house at a quarter to twelve with the money still in the trunk. He got in the car, and we started off to the track. As I turned on to the 134, I said, casually, "How come you didn't get her the De Soto?"

He darkened and turned away for a moment. Then he said, through his teeth, "There never was any De Soto."

"That's what she said."

"She couldn't get off the De Soto for one goddamn minute. I come home, and she's sitting around in a housedress smoking Chesterfields and listening to Stella Dallas. I say, 'What'd you do today?' And she says, 'Where's my De Soto?'"

"You never promised her a De Soto?"

He didn't answer. We drove in silence for a few miles before he said, "A man comes home he wants a little peace and quiet. A highball, maybe something to eat. He likes to see a woman in a nice dress, smelling good from the bath. You put something on the Victrola, put your feet up, have some conversation. You don't want to hear about no De Soto from a woman in a housedress smoking Chesterfields."

Edgar bet chalk all day and cashed forty-eight dollars worth of tickets. We drove home talking about the horses. When we were in front of his house, I asked, "If she didn't treat you well, why do you want to buy her a car?"

He looked at me like I had just asked the dumbest question in the world.

"That's the only way to shut her up."

"She's not talking to you anymore. She doesn't even know where you live. You don't have a telephone. How can she talk to you?"

"You kidding? That woman hasn't shut her mouth in nearly sixty years," he said, with venom. And then he got out of the car and walked to his house.

At four o'clock that morning I woke up from a sound sleep with the solution. As Edgar said, you didn't have to win the race as long as you made the right bet.

I waited for the paper to be delivered at six. There were ads for a couple of places in Orange County off the 405. By nine I was dressed and heading south.

The fourth dealer I went to had one. I took the title in the name of my mother, Frances Bidden. They agreed to deliver it to Navy Street the following day at 3 P.M. Prepped, lubed, and washed.

They were only ten minutes late. They parked it right in front of Frances and Eunice's house. I took the keys, signed the delivery papers, tipped the guys two hundred dollars of Edgar's money.

As soon as they were gone, I went up to the sunporch and knocked. It took a while for Frances Bidden to answer. When she did, she saw a 1937 teal and gray De Soto with white-wall tires and galvanized-rubber running boards parked in front of her house.

I tossed her the keys and said, "Don't pull the choke out all the way when you start her or you'll flood it."

She just stood there, her face filling with color.

"That son of a bitch," she whispered through her teeth.

I never told Edgar what I'd done. And he never asked. He just assumed I'd taken care of it, and I had. It was over. It took nearly sixty years, but it was finally over.

Edgar died that winter. In January. Just after the season

opened at Santa Anita. When I showed up one Wednesday a neighbor told me he had collapsed with a massive coronary on Hollywood Boulevard.

It took me a while to track down the body. It was in the morgue downtown in the section for people who die with no next of kin, awaiting cremation at county expense.

There was a little less than four grand left in the Lufthansa bag. Enough for a middle-of-the-line casket and a plot at a landfill cemetery in the Valley. When I called Frances Bidden to ask if she wanted to say good-bye to Edgar, she hung up on me.

So on a Friday morning in January I stood alone at the graveside watching them lower Edgar into the ground. A fine rain started to fall. It would be a good day for mudders. As the dirt hit the side of the coffin, I wondered if I would die as happy as Edgar Dent.

Daniel Villasenor

This picture has haunted me all my life. I was six, but I didn't look like that at six. It took me twenty years to even begin to resemble it. Everyone has a picture like this. As if it knows already the mysterious purpose of your life. I still check back with it, from time to time, to see how I'm coming along.

Daniel Villasenor lives in Taos, New Mexico, and makes his living as a blacksmith and a horse trainer. He also teaches the martial and medical art of Qigong, as well as an English class on the Taos Pueblo. For most of his writing life he has been a poet. He has an MFA in poetry.

DANIEL VILLASENOR
Wendell's Singing

FIRST-PLACE WINNER
Short-Story Award
for New Writers

he was always reading. It was Wyoming, but it was
the month of May and weirdly warm, and Wendell was tall,
and when he rose to pay he leaned into the counter. And
because the lights above the register were concentrated track
lights, he could see that through the pale yellow cotton of her
dress, under the book in her lap, she wore no underwear. She
never wore underwear. Her hair was not blond, but he guessed
it was blonder than it was; it looked always like it had been
washed last week and combed two days ago. So it was light
brown, and her eyes were a shade browner, the color of wheat
toast just before it begins to burn. She had four or five yet-
darker hairs directly between her eyebrows, which went in
various directions that changed from week to week, sometimes thrust in one direction as if, with a sudden strenuous
thought, she had jammed the heel of her hand to her brow; and
sometimes they were simply frozen in a chaos unfigureable.
Her skin was slightly dry, as if a thimbleful of moisture could
restore it for a day. As if a little oil on the end of Wendell's
pinkie could color her. Her neck was thin and the radius that
gave on to the shoulders was gradual, the shoulders delicate and
slightly pointy, which gave her an air of fragile formality when
she sat. Her throat was prominent and long, the skin over it

nearly translucent, two blue veins visible on the left side, the side turned toward customers, which disappeared into the shadow beneath the angle of her jaw. And her chin came around in a curve, the easy shape, Wendell thought, of the gesture a girl's hand makes in the air trying to recapture blown spores. Her mouth had about it the color of red-suddenly-departed, as if it held within it the memory of flushing, and now it was shut down, temporarily closed. There were vertical lines visible in both lips, neither dry nor wet, and a flake of paler skin on her bottom lip which she bit.

She never looked at anyone. She seemed afraid of what she might find in people's faces. When she rose to go outside to smoke the entire restaurant turned to watch her. Because she moved vaguely leonine in her pale yellow dress. And because she moved in an attitude altogether unobserved, as a woman clad in a nightgown in her own home moves across her room to turn off a light. No one had seen a woman like her behind the counter at Rita's. She had been working the register for three weeks and Wendell had never seen her look at anyone. She did look at his left arm. When he paid he watched her eyes. Wendell was a welder. It had always been a joke: Wendell the welder. His left arm was full of small, fiery red holes and the steak-colored smooth scars of older holes. So that it looked diseased. But only his left arm. He was strong and wiry and tall and his arms and hands were thicker and more muscular, proportionately, than the rest of his body, which was slight, so that it was hard to notice anything about him but for his arms and hands. And his face. He carried a permanent expression of disingenuous and responsible sorrow, as if he were forever on the verge of having to close down a business whose employees were his family and friends of long standing, and who depended on him for their welfare. But it didn't make him look deprecating. It made him look durable, the way grief can.

His jaw was solid and heavy, his nose was strong and bent

gradually downward from the bridge, which gave his countenance an association with ships, with difficult travel. His mouth was ample. And the lines around his mouth and eyes were intense, his skin was tanned and leathery from tacking welds without a helmet. He was balding, but what hair he had was thick and of a rich brown that bordered on red. He wore, always, the same soot-spattered and welding-burnt golden brown Carhartt overalls and a V-neck T-shirt, the sleeves of which, in the uncanny heat, he kept rolled up and notched above his biceps. She counted out his change and said to his arm, Thank you, please come back.

And because she never looked at anyone, he strained to hear what she might say to others. He sat close to the entrance of Rita's. He heard her say thank you a hundred times. And he told himself one Tuesday (Tuesday was the one night he made the trip to town to eat out and shower at the gym) that if for two more Tuesdays he did not hear her say please come back to a single other customer, he would ask her what she was reading. What she was always reading. Which terrified him. Because Wendell never read.

What are you reading?

It was nearly nine o'clock. He had gnawed his bones as the place slowly emptied.

She looked first around the room as if someone in the kitchen or at a far table had asked for her assistance; then she took an index finger and marked her place, and with the other she put some loose hair behind each ear.

A book. *The Heart Is a Lonely Hunter.*

Is it good?

I think so. I think it is.

What's it about?

It's about two friends. They're strange, deformed. And a girl. It's a dark book really. It's terrible.

Wendell made a subtle ducking motion with his head, as if

84

by the slight slipstream of this movement he might lift her chin and make her meet his eyes. Which is exactly what happened.

Do you want to smoke? he asked her.

Yes.

They went outside, and when he just stood with his hands looped in the side openings of his overalls she offered him a cigarette, and he said no, and she looked at him, a corner of her mouth lifting.

I don't smoke, he said.

You don't smoke.

No. Everything I do is unhealthy. At work. So I figure to do what I can.

Why did you ask me if I wanted to smoke?

Forgive me, he said. I like to watch you smoke.

Oh, she said.

There was a long pause, her long slow exhale, and the puddle of breath after.

Why? she said.

Because—

No, she said. I have to close out.

She looked at him. The register, she said.

I'll see you next time, he said.

Yes.

Wendell tried to come earlier and he always stayed later. On Tuesdays at lunch he told Marv he had to get to town by six before the bank closed, or the post office, or UPS, or whatever he could think of. At Rita's he ordered the same meal every time. Half a barbecued chicken, two breasts, each with a wing, and the salad bar. For fifty bucks a month he lived behind Teton Welding in a trailer the size of most master-bedroom bathrooms, without electricity or water, and he heated with propane and an element. He lit the place with one kerosene lantern hanging from a horseshoe welded to the ceiling. He told himself and anyone who asked that he cooked on a Coleman stove, but the suction pump leaked and had to be pumped over two hundred times before it would ignite, and after ten hours at the shop he usually fell on his bed and tipped the cold Progresso soup right out of the can.

And at Rita's he would sit over his plate and let the rising steam open his pores. And after he had devoured one piece of chicken, he would look at her until she looked up from her book at him, and then he would smile and bend back to his plate to eat. He imagined that if he looked at her with enough collected energy, enough intent, that he could magically lift her chin, and she would meet his eyes. His meals lasted three hours. Six thirty to nine thirty. On the third Tuesday after he had asked her what she was reading, he was staring at her, trying with a large portion of his will to make her face lift from the pages of her book, when she did, suddenly, look at him. And just as suddenly she laughed.

He stood up. He walked over to the counter and leaned there, and, repressing laughter himself, he said, What are you reading?

Gray's Anatomy.

What?

Gray's Anatomy. It's a medical textbook. I'm looking at my father's lung.

Wendell saw the huge gray book. He hadn't looked to her lap when he had asked what she was reading. He had been watching the lines around her mouth to see the play in them, to see the subtle attenuations that he wanted to believe were invitations. She had three lines on either side of her mouth, vertical crescents that played about quietly when her mouth moved even slightly. As if these lines were themselves cajolers to the serious mouth. Coaxers.

That is a huge book, he said. Your father's lung. Let me see your father's lung. How did your father's lung find its way into that book?

He's dying of cancer. That's why I'm here. This is what his lung looks like.

She turned the book towards Wendell. He smoked for fifty years.

Where is he?

Moran Junction.

There's no hospital in Moran.

I know. There's nothing to do at this point but be there with him. He's alone. He used to work at the plant. It won't be long. Anyhow.

Where did you come from? Wendell said.

She looked again to the double swinging doors of the kitchen, but it was late, and the cooks were in the back lot smoking and drinking, and their laughter could be heard coming through the door which they'd propped with a dairy crate. And the air coming through Rita's was warm and tinged with cigarette smoke and grease, and the wind brought a wetness also as it came and mixed with the smell of barbecue off the grill, and Wendell took a deep breath and looked out the front window where the late sun or the early moon made heavy the dark blue susserations of clouds, and he looked down into the shadows of her loins where the pale yellow dress plummeted, and, Wait, he said, what is your name?

Catharine. I'm Catharine.

Wendell, Wendell said. Wendell the welder.

She laughed. The second time. When she laughed she spurted laughter. Not that she was polite or ashamed, not that she was ladylike in her laughter. But it was as if every time she laughed a soft, trapped thing—a thing was how Wendell imagined it—escaped from her mouth, from her chest and lungs, and at the last second she tried to swallow it back in. Not from propriety, but because it might be lost. He even saw himself retrieving this thing, standing on his toes to reach it above the pot racks, crawling on his knees under the tables.

What do you weld?

Where did you come from?

Los Angeles.

Los Angeles! Christ.

Yes, I know.

What the hell were you doing in Los Angeles?

I am in med school. I was in med school. At UCLA.

Med school. You're a doctor?

I was halfway.

She stood and looked at him. It's a beautiful night. I want to sit outside for a moment and smoke.

But he didn't move. He was looking at her mouth, so that when the lines began to tremble a little he addressed them. She's a doctor, he said, to the lines; they trembled in a dance. Did you know that she was a doctor?

He took to eating quickly. He'd finish and go to the men's room, and study his face briefly to see what she might find there, and then he would stand to the side of the counter and listen to her tell him the plots of her books. He stood slightly bent in such a way as he never stood, and he listened with great gravity as if he might come to understand something he'd missed of the way things were in the world. And when he listened he could not look at her, because he could not hear her for the involuntary quivers of her mouth, or the sudden silent draft of her gaze, at once limpid and resigned, as if it came from loneliness and returned to loneliness, and carried all it held back to loneliness; and not a loneliness all her own, but a comprehensive loneliness that made him want a sentience for all things, like a man come back from great illness or a war.

Now he had laid down newspaper and the two of them were on their backs looking up at the underside of one of the huge bench tables in Rita's Lounge. The sign that said Best Barbecue in Town was dark. Everyone had gone home. The front door was locked, but the back door was propped open as the cooks had left it. It was after ten o'clock. The only sounds were the whirs of the freezers and the refrigerators, and the oceanic swooshes of late cars out on the wet road.

When I was a child, Wendell said, we had a breasty babysitter named Susan Luca—I think it was Luca—and we played that same old game where you hide and she has to find you. And I remember we had a day bed that was high off the ground, about the height of this table, only it had a dirty cloth ruffle around it. And I always hid under there, which was really stupid. I mean, the point was to hide. But I guess that wasn't the point. Because I'd lie there, and I'd hear her, and I'd see her pink slippers in the inch of space between the ruffle and the rug, and I would begin to breathe in a crazy kind of pattern, and my heart would pound so loud I swear I was afraid it would crack my ribs. And she would walk around saying, Hmmm, I know he must be somewhere, and all the while my breath would be crazier and crazier and then suddenly, just when I thought she had waited too long and finally given up the game, she'd whip up the ruffle and say, Gotcha! And every time I would piss my pants. Every time. I can't believe I'm telling you this.

Catharine laughed, her shoulders shaking. Do you have to go to the bathroom?

No. Thank you.

He put his finger on the seam where a piece of angle iron met the two-inch frame tubing. This is a shitter, we say. A kid out of high school, greener than grass. It looks like bunches of gum under spray paint. Now look down here.

He slid his hand down one of the legs to where it sloped

gently into the mane of an iron lion's head. And this, he said, moving his finger back and forth across the gentle, barely perceptible waves of the joint. This is a journeyman weld. Touch it. You can't even see it's welded. You have to touch it. The little dip in it.

Catharine put her hand on it, and he told her to close her eyes, and she did.

I can't feel a thing.

Yes you can. Move your hand up the leg and run it down again.

He put his hand over hers. Slowly, he said.

Tell me when we hit the weld, he said, in her ear.

Now, she said. There. Am I right? Can I open my eyes?

No, he said.

That's not it? I think that has to be it.

Yes, that's it. But don't open your eyes.

He was watching the blood pump in the veins of her neck. He had never wanted to touch anything so badly. It had been nearly three years since he had been with a woman. He thought that he might be a clumsy lover. But he had the feeling as he lay there with his breath held and his heart pounding that if he touched her neck she would come. Or cry. Her color had risen. Her hand was sweating. He took his hand off hers and put his middle and index fingers together, and brought them so they nearly grazed her neck, the diminutive pulsings there that seemed to him as tangible as if they were already tears.

Wendell, she said softly. Can I open my eyes?

He moved his hand. Yes, he said.

It was late June now, late of a Tuesday night, and neither of them cared how late. They had taken to sitting on the porch at Rita's in the clear night air. In the dusky light from the premature moon they could see vaguely the upper half of some of the Teton range in snow. All the shops across were long closed, and their silent, darkened figures and wares gave off a solitude to the street, as did the sound of the thick tires of the last cruising pickups on the wet road, which would not dry until August if it did dry at all.

They had been silent for a long time, and then she had leaned her head into his shoulder so that he could smell her hair, which smelled of eucalyptus and cigarette smoke, and the wet, alluvial beds of the creeks he used to play in as a boy, and a shock had gone into his hip and remained there so that he felt he had to move or speak.

I'll give you a year and you tell me a story. From your life.

You're brave, she said.

Nineteen seventy-eight.

Why that year?

I have no idea.

My mother finally left him that year. Or kicked him out. We were in Wilmot, Nebraska. She was a secretary at an insurance firm, and he transferred to Moran. His truck was running and he came back in and grabbed all the beer in the fridge. I'm surely going to need this now, I'm surely going to need this now, he said, so close to my mother's face that he was spitting on her. She quit her job. It was December. She quit her job when we needed the money most.

She sat up and lit a cigarette.

I remember her standing in the kitchen and throwing plates. One after another between her feet. That Christmas was spent on my knees cleaning up after her. This is a grim game, Wendell the welder.

You stayed there?

No. She got a job waitressing at a truck stop. She met a man named Bill who said he owned a restaurant and bar actually called Wild Bill's Hangout, in Ville Platte, Louisiana. In a small town. She didn't believe him—she had some sense, my mother. So he offered to fly her out to see it, and if she wanted to stay she could, and if she didn't he'd just fly her back. She came home and said, We're moving to Ville Platte.

Was he a good man?

He was a very good man. He was a retired amateur boxer among other things, and he'd become kind of a radical pacifist. In magic marker on the walls of the bar he wrote things like Anyone Caught Fighting Will Be Disallowed From Entering Again, and Belligerence Will Not Be Tolerated In This Bar. And he had such a reputation as a fighter, however many years ago, that people were scared of him. He was funny. He was the mailman too, just to get out and visit with people. He'd walk it. He had a huge handlebar mustache and he wore cowboy boots and a Stetson. I think he saved my mother's life.

She turned and looked at him. So I came of age in a bar in Ville Platte, Louisiana.

He looked at her neck, which flurried in small spasms when she breathed. When she was looked at.

Is that enough? she said.

No.

That spring I turned fourteen. I didn't know anyone. My friends were the men at the bar, Bill's friends. School was my refuge. I should say perfection was my refuge. I was sick, I think. I mean, there were some years I didn't miss a single question on any of my tests. For a whole year. And I read. I read all the time.

I believe you, Wendell said.

When I look back on it I think I had the feeling that my life was closing in on me. It was a suffocation, the provinciality of it, my life. I ate Caesar salads while everyone ate crawdads. I felt like all the adults around me—I had no friends my age—I felt like they were in a conspiracy to make me bland. So I read with a violence to spite them.

She paused and bit her lip.

I like to hear you talk, he said. The way you talk.

I wiped down glasses behind the bar and I put out peanuts and popcorn. I got good at darts. I was nearly unbeatable, but for this man named TooTall. He'd say, Cat, you look like you need to throw a knife at someone you can't miss. And I'd say, Indeed. Indeed always made him howl with laughter. He'd say, What did you say, Cat? and I'd say, I said indeed, and I'd enunciate it and he'd almost fall off his stool with laughter. Then we'd play darts, sometimes until we were the only ones left in the bar.

She stopped. She lifted one leg and pointed it, and folded it back underneath the bench. And that spring I began to hate my mother. Hating my mother at fourteen was probably the only normal thing that ever happened in my childhood. She was the reason I was perfect in school. To spite her. My mother hated my mind. And the more I felt her hatred, the more I studied.

And medicine?

I was the only girl in the class who would cut things open. I'd slice open the frogs and hurl them at the boys. They called me Formaldehyda.

She laughed and leaned forward, and rubbed her temples with the heel of her hands. Your turn. I'm tired.

I don't know, Catharine. I'm a welder. I've had one life for fifteen years.

I don't believe you.

It's so.

Okay. Before that.

Before that I was dreaming of you.

No, she said. No. Tell me something.

Give me a year.

Nineteen seventy-two.

I was fourteen.

You're thirty-seven?

I'm thirty-seven. Don't get me wrong. My father was the sourest son of a bitch I've ever known. But I'll tell you something. I worked at a deli called Spanky's after school, and he let me off early one day, and I was surprised to see my father's Chevy in front of the house. It was one of those kit mobile houses, and frankly I was scared because anything out of routine with him meant anything bad. And I crept in quietly and called out to him, and nothing, and I went to the kitchen, and nothing, and I went to take a piss in the bathroom, which was in the back, and I looked out the window, and I saw him kneeling out in the dirt behind the scrap heap, on some huge, circular army-green tarp, and it looked like he was pulling it apart. But I looked closer and saw that he was sewing. I didn't even know that he could sew. I went outside. What are you doing? I said. Get back in the house, Wendell, you stupid son of a bitch, he said, I got you something.

And when he came back in he looked like he'd been drinking, but I knew he hadn't been because he was moving quickly, and he never moved quickly when he drank. Get in the car, he said, we're going to the high school. My dad played cards with the guys at the firehouse sometimes, so it was nothing unusual to pull by there, because we did a lot. And he went in and came out with an eight-foot ladder and put it in the back of the truck, and said, Come on, as if I wasn't just sitting there already in the truck waiting for him. That's when I knew he was excited. When he was sober and he didn't make any sense.

At the high school there was a water tower that supplied all the water to Leeton—that's the town where I grew up. It was the tallest thing in the six towns we called The Valley. And my dad drove right over the grounds and the practice football field to the base of the water tower, and we got out and he said, We're going up, and he reached around my body and tied on a harness, and he yanked me by the arm and said, You want to, don't you? and I said yes. I had no idea what we were doing.

Oh god, Catharine said.

No, wait, it gets better.

So he propped the ladder against the bottom of the perma-nent bolted-in rungs that ran all the way up the tower—there was a twelve-foot drop-off so kids wouldn't do exactly what we were doing—and we climbed up. Don't look down, he said, and I didn't.

When we got to the top, he spread the tarp out and made me stand on one end of it because of the wind until he could get it sorted out. And the wind, good lord,was wind. I mean it was hard to stand. He called me over and he attached a bunch of ropes and cables to my harness, and he said, Son—he hardly ever called me son—he said, Son, this here is a parachute. I bought it at the surplus store. I'm going to give you the time of your life. And we walked to the edge, and he held the massive folds of the thing in his arms behind me, and, Wendell, he yelled, jump! And I did. I don't remember the feeling, but my body does. I mean, I know it was the greatest thing that I had ever felt, it still is. And at times I dream it again, and I can feel it in my body when I dream. What I do remember is the sound of my father whooping and yelling as I flew. What I have of it now is that perfect blue sky, and my father's hoarse curses and cheers. And I landed, and I tumbled, and I remember laying there on the earth, with one thought only, which was that I had to do it again and again, and he came up running, whooping and hollering and yelling, Beauty, motherfucking beauty! And I said, Can I do it again? and he stopped suddenly. He looked right at me and said, Are you crazy? You're liable to kill yourself.

That happened in 1972.

Catharine had her dress clenched in both hands. She stood up and sat down again and smoothed the places where her hands had been. Wendell, she said.

And then she leaned forward in that gesture, with the heels of her hands grinding the thin skin around her temples and grinding the wisps of fine hair, made even stranger and more animate by the warmth and the humidity of the air.

I cannot believe, she said. I cannot believe that you might be who I think you are.

How is he?

He was a bastard to me all my life. Really, he was a drunk. It's strange how things end up. I mean, you put up and put up as a girl, and then you spend fifteen years trying to undo the damage you've done to yourself by all that putting up, and then suddenly you're thirty-one and he's dying, and you're cooking for him and reading him to sleep.

She blew out a slow stream of smoke. It was the first Tuesday in July, and the light in the evening seemed nearly interminable. Wendell was spooning potato salad from a two-quart tub. He looked up at the mountains. I can't believe there's still snow at six thousand feet. What damage?

Nothing sexual, if that's what you mean. He hit me. A few times hard. Three. Three times.

No, you said damage to yourself.

Oh, that. That's boring. That's the mountain of shit you plow through when your dad's drunk, and you spend the rest of your life telling other people whose dads were drunk what you've been through, and you're supposed to marry against your will a man just like your drunk dad, and it's a pile of never-ending horseshit.

I see, Wendell said. My father hit me all the time. The summer I was thirteen it got so bad, I remember in the mornings looking in the mirror to see which side of me was less bruised up, so I'd know which side to turn to him when he came at me. But people cry about that stuff all the time. I'm not saying you. Good lord, not you.

He put his hand on her thigh. He left it there.

I think it's a little different with girls, he said. I mean, my dad was a piece of shit too, don't get me wrong. But there've been times, more than a few, when I've been grateful. I mean, stuff happens at the shop all the time. Not all the time. Now and again. People get in your face. And it's not good to always turn the other cheek. Sometimes it is. But it's a different world in shops. Just like horses or whatever, there's a hierarchy, and even if your heart is good, you have to hold your own. And if you've been hit all your kid life then you're not afraid of anyone. It helps.

You're not afraid of anyone?

Oh, I'm afraid of some. I'm terrified of you.

She made a fist in her lap and looked at it, and said, All right, and smiled. And then she inhaled deeply and let the warmth sit in her lungs, and she let it out in languid clouds about her face, and she did not wave it away. He was studying her. Why do you like to watch me smoke? she said.

I don't know. Because it's wrong. Because you're taking something dangerous all the way into your body and letting it stay there. As long as it pleases you. Even if it's killing you. Just because you like it. Because it makes me think that you don't believe you can heal all the sick just because you're a doctor. Because you know down here we just pick a thing and do it the best we can. Welding, medicine. But anything can happen, anytime. It's a moment's pleasure. It's a Fuck you, Death. At the shop I say that everyday of my life.

He looked at her mouth. Because it's oral.

She rubbed the butt into the bench. He's dead, your dad?

Cancer. Lung, too. But it went everywhere. It was some shit

they used at the mill. He didn't smoke.

Your mom?

She died in a car wreck. When I was five.

She turned to him. The deepest line in his face ran from the flesh at the crook in the side of his nose to the corner of his mouth, and she put her finger into it and dug deeply with her nail, and ran it slowly down the groove as if she were cutting him open. He kept his eyes on her eyes and he did not flinch, and when she reached his mouth he took her finger between his teeth and he bit her. Hard. She breathed in quickly. He sucked her finger where he knew he'd hurt her.

Wendell, she said. I am not teasing you. We will make love. I swear to you. I'm going to drive home now. I am only frightened.

She reached her free hand under her dress and moved it there, and brought it out, and with her drenched fingers she closed the lids of his eyes.

All week at work he was as another man entire. Marv called him in and said, What the hell's the matter with you?

Is my work all right?

Your work is good, it's always good. What the hell's the matter with you? You're manic. The guys are afraid you're going to hit 'em. Or kiss 'em. Christ, nobody can get near you.

I don't know, Wendell said, lifting his eyebrows and letting them fall several times in succession.

Christ, Marv said.

My work is good?

Your work is good.

All right, Wendell said.

But on Friday night he had the dream. In the dream he had been ill for nearly three years, and he felt a great hebetude in his body, and he was driving his jeep down an increasingly corroded road. And the jeep kept tilting downward in a sensation of quicksand thickening, and this in proportion to his own lethargy, and he had to wake himself up so as not to drive himself into the earth. And in order to do this he was singing, in a strange drunken voice that was barely his own. And there appeared before him suddenly a lake, and a stand with some kids selling lemonade in the sunshine. The lemonade, in his mind, took on the quality of an elixir, and he approached the children, but they grew slowly terrified of him. And the stand seemed to recede even as he approached it, and it was only with a tremendous effort of the damaged singing that, exhausted, he came within reach of a single paper cup. And he reached for it and he touched its rim, but then he fell. He fell and the huge figure of his father was standing over him, and his chest was opened in a wound, and he said, You want to float? You want to float? And he reached into his own riven body and pulled out a wet stack of green algae and viscera-coated sheets, and Wendell saw that they were lily pads. Float, his father said. You wretched motherfucker, float.

He woke and tore at the sheets. He knew that Catharine's father was dead, and that he didn't know who she was, and that she was leaving Wyoming, and that he loved her. These things came to him in the same instant. He walked outside. Lights from the garage played on the mounds of scrap metal, the tractors, the abandoned cars, and in the same sallow light which gave off the pale siding of the shop, he could see three stray dogs gnawing on some bones at the north end of the lot. The old, broken trip-hammer lay on its side in the spring mud like a huge, slain dinosaur.

To the pale, corrugated, broad side of the shop, Let me, he said, have her. Let me have her.

He looked up at the sky and he breathed in deeply, as if to inhale some fortitude from those distant, nameless suns. And he opened and closed his hands, and he looked down at the earth, and at the yard around. Look at this mess. Let me have her. If she is leaving, let her want to take me. If she is staying, let her want to stay with me.

He had not asked for anything since he had asked for a power to kill his father. He had lied to Catharine. Because he wanted only the present. He suspected memory. He hated nostalgia. But he could have murdered the old man himself. And he was not thankful for the beatings. He was thankful for the food his father gave him, and the roof over his head, and the time that had passed until he was a man. Until he could leave.

Let me, he said. And he went inside and slept.

On Tuesday he drove to town repeating a grim refrain: It was just the dream, it was just the dream. But she was gone. She was gone. He knew it even before he looked, but the sight of a girl in her chair made him stumble with sickness. He sat. He ordered. And Gloria, who was the head cook, brought his dish out herself in what seemed to him a matter of seconds. She leaned over and looked at him. She left this with me for you.

She pulled an envelope out of her apron, and put her hand quickly on the back of his head, and turned to the kitchen.

Wendell pushed his plate out of the way and put the envelope where it had been. He broke the seal and opened it and read:

> Wendell,
>
> He's gone, and I cried, but not for him. When I said that I was only afraid, it was for you. For you. You have no idea who I am. I am foul, Wendell. I have been with many too many men. I did not want you to be one of them. To be another. I am cleaning my body. Every day I wake up and I am a day cleaner. You make me want to be clean. Never before have I wanted to be so clean. I think you are a saint. I have been, nearly, a whore. You are the first man I have ever wanted to make love to. I didn't think I could feel

that longing. How can I thank you for this? Blessed man, I am so sorry.

Catharine

It was forty-six and a half miles to his trailer. It was ten minutes before seven o'clock. The sun was setting and coming through the windows. It gave the maple trim in Rita's Lounge the intensity of a blaze. Motes—motes and the swirling meat smoke from the grill. The clanging of dishes, and the laughter of the cooks, and a baby crying, and some utensil falling, and the turning of the hot meat in the grease. The ring of the register.

Get up, he said to himself. Get up and go home.

He climbed into his jeep and drove. He rolled the window down. He felt that he might throw up. He crossed the Snake River glinting in the sun, and he passed the Astoria Springs; and he passed through the Hoback Range, with the western light flooding the valley, and the peaks of the mountains, and the graceful, glacier-like curves of the lower hills. And he saw broad swaths in the mud where the elk had been, and down in the Hoback he saw anglers up to their waists in the runoff, and the blinding firmament off the rapids in the last tangent rays of the sun.

He drove slowly. By the time he made the lot it was nearly dark. He pulled alongside the trailer and sat with the engine running, as if to turn it off and to get out was to begin something he did not want to begin. He turned the key and he stepped out of the jeep, and he walked toward the shop. He went in and pulled the eight-pound sledge off the rack. He came back out and closed the door, and the dogs ceased their gnawing and looked at him from across the lot. What are you looking at? he said.

He walked to the trailer and he began to swing. Silently at first, and then his grunts filled the empty lot like a man dying.

He swung hard and the aluminum gave way easily, and he turned the head of the hammer sideways and swung harder, so that the whole side began to cave in, and, Dirty motherfucker, he yelled, You dirty motherfucker, and he went around the backside and smashed the window, and began again freshly on the north side, striking deep, dull blows into the siding. And then he heard someone singing. He stopped, the hammer in the air. And the singing stopped. He swung again and the singing began, and now he swung like a machine, and the singing grew louder, and he saw the spit flying from his own mouth, and he realized that it was he who was singing. The same drunken, unintelligible song of the dream, and he stood trembling.

Breathe, he said. You crazy son of a gun, breathe.

And he did. When he could hear the sound of the dogs' teeth on the bones he let the hammer fall. He went inside the trailer, and, ducking under the jagged edges of wrecked siding, he took his bag of toiletries, an envelope with cash, and some jeans and shirts and underwear, and stuffed them in a duffel. He also took his three pairs of overalls and his boots, and pushed it all by the door, and ducked down and crawled out over them, and put them in the back of his jeep. He started the engine and then he just sat. He got out and went back in, and pulled from the wall above the bowl which was his sink a small, toothpaste-splattered mirror which hung by a wire from a nail.

He walked across to the shop and went in and found his three helmets, and his gloves, and the expensive plasma tips he'd bought and hidden for his own use. I have to tell Marv, he thought.

He made a note in his mind, and he walked into Marv's office and wrote it:

Marv,

I'm thirty-seven years old. I have a chunk of money in the bank.

I'm going to buy some land. With a river. I'm going to fish and bathe in the same goddamned river.

Wendell

He walked out into the night. Not a sound but the low engine of the jeep, and the air he took in and let go. In the peripheral glow from the taillight, he could see the corrupted outline of his trailer, like some alien shrapnel waste come to perfection in the desolate yard. He looked up at the sky, which was nearly purple to the east, and laced with garnet trailings in the west. When, on what day, will you learn to weep? he said.

SHORT-STORY AWARD FOR NEW WRITERS
1st-, 2nd-, and 3rd-Place Winners

•◦ *1st place* and $1200 to *Daniel Villasenor*, for "Wendell's Singing"
Villasenor's profile appears on page 80 and his story begins on page 81.

•◦ *2nd place* and $500 to *Calvin Wright*, for "Mr. and Mrs. Fred Wood"
Calvin Wright is an undergraduate at Yale University and lives in upstate New York.

Calvin Wright
Calvin Wright
"Mr. and Mrs. Fred Wood"
Mrs. Betty Wood died while she was cooking breakfast. It was fried eggs over-easy with a side of twin, Jimmy Dean sausage links, drowned in maple syrup. Fred Wood was in the living room, waiting for his meal.

•◦ *3rd place* and $300 to *Paula Yoo*, for "Closer to Home"
Paula Yoo, a *People* magazine staff correspondent and former *Seattle Times* and *Detroit News* reporter, holds degrees from Yale and Columbia University. She was a 1997 finalist for the James Kirkwood Creative Writing Award at the UCLA Writers' Program. She lives in Los Angeles and is working on a novel.

Paula Yoo
Paula Yoo
"Closer to Home"
We left soon after; the noise and smoke were too much for my father. I didn't know at the time that those four words, "Nice to meet you," would be his only words to Mark. I wonder if Mark believed him.

We thank all entrants for sending in their work.

ALBERTO RÍOS
Poet

Interview

by Susan McInnis

Alberto Ríos is Regents Professor of English at Arizona State University at Tempe. He has published four books of poetry: Whispering to Fool the Wind *in 1982 (for which he was given the Walt Whitman Award),* Five Indiscretions *in 1985, and* Lime Orchard Woman *in 1988, all from Sheep Meadow, and* Teodoro Luna's Two Kisses *in 1990, from W.W. Norton. His two books of short fiction are* The Iguana Killer *in 1984 (for which he received the Western States Book Award for fiction), from Confluence Press, and* Pig Cookies *in 1995, from Chronicle Books. A reissue of* The Iguana Killer *is forthcoming from the University of New Mexico Press. His work has earned five Pushcart Prizes in poetry and fiction, inclusion in* The Norton Anthology of Modern Poetry, *as well as publication in more than a hundred other national and international anthologies. Ríos is the recent recipient of the Arizona Governor's Arts Award. Other honors include fellowships from Guggenheim, the NEA, and ASU Graduate College.*

Alberto Ríos

Photo credit Marla A. Davey

Glimmer Train Stories, Issue 26, Spring 1998
© *1997 Susan McInnis*

MCINNIS: You grew up in Nogales, Arizona—cheek-to-jowl with Nogales, Sonora, Mexico. Were you growing up with a foot in each culture?

RÍOS: For me, it's more than straddling two cultures. It's really three. There is an in-between state, a very messy, wonderful middleness to the culture I come from. It is a culture of capillaries, a culture of exchange, of the small detail that is absorbed the way oxygen enters blood. On the border we're dealing with several languages, several cultures, different sets of laws, and everything else you can imagine. Nevertheless, you've got to live side-by-side. What results isn't neatly anybody's law, anybody's language. It's more a third way of living, and that time, or place of exchange, reckons with the world a little differently.

Is it a place where divisions break down?

They have to break down. Otherwise you're just like two animals butting against each other, and you don't live that way. That's how you fight. And I think that wasn't what we were doing.

It seems that way by some measures. The fence across the border is an example. But it's a silly fence. When I was a boy, there were holes all over it. You could go anywhere along the fence and see where it was cut. And even now, if you stand at the border you see people running wildly across the hillsides going from one country to the other. So that part's pretty silly. But the fence—now a wall—is there.

I grew up with it, but my sense of place has a lot to do with the stories I heard, not just the things I lived through. In their stories, my great aunts and grandmother talk about a time *sin linea*, "without a line," a time of hillsides and of people: a time of manners, where you just don't cross into somebody else's yard, and you live by that understanding.

You've said that, as you grew up, your first language wasn't really Spanish, and wasn't really English, but was a language of listening.

What does that mean to you?

Well, it was, again, a language of manners. In the mix of cultures I grew up in, children were first and always told to "be quiet." That would seem to be restrictive—a punishment—but, in fact, it wasn't. It was how they were teaching us that first language of listening: "Be quiet!" It's not a terrible thing to hear.

In that quietude we were able to hear with both ears. And also with the eyes and with the nose and with everything else we had. I mean, we had two ears—which was very convenient. We had one for each language. And then, the nose for the smells of cooking, and so on. And I think the great mix of things made listening all we could do. We couldn't talk very well. It wasn't something we were capable of when we were being inundated with so much. We were simply, I think, positioning ourselves, so we could have something to say and be a player as we grew a little older, when it was appropriate in that culture to have something to say.

This sometimes was perceived as a negative thing in the classroom. We were told to be quiet by our parents as we went to school. Our teachers might have tried to say things like, "Just ask! Just ask!" but we didn't understand how to do that. We knew how to listen, and that was our way of learning.

This is the Mexican kid, the border kid.

Very much. Very much. At least as I was growing up.

Were you absorbing?

I think we were working a little harder than that. I remember, in second grade, getting in some trouble—even though I was a good student. I was doing all the homework and finishing everything on time, but my parents were called to the school because I got caught committing that heinous crime of daydreaming. I think now that's probably when I was starting to be a writer. I was not simply absorbing. I was engaging. I was putting all that stuff together in some way and projecting. And to get into trouble for it! You know, I think school was set up to give you information, but they forget that at some point, you learn how to do something with it.

As a child, a second-grader, all you can do is daydream. All you can do is imagine how to put it all together. There should have been a reward, but we don't know how to reward daydreaming. And so, I think that "quiet," in a school setting, can sometimes be perceived as a negative thing and it shouldn't be. Not if you're doing all the other things they want you to do.

A related question: In this day and age, we would say, "How good that Alberto speaks two languages!" But in the early '50s?

Very different, very different. In fact, language was effectively taken away from us. We came to the first-grade classroom, and rather than hearing, "Congratulations, we're so glad you can speak these languages," the first thing we were told was, "You can't speak Spanish here!"

We all looked at each other, and that seemed a very strange observation about us. So we raised our hands, and said, "*Seguro que sí!* Of course, we can speak Spanish!"

The teacher said, "That's not what we mean. We mean, you are not to speak Spanish here, and if you do, we are going to swat you." And, in fact, we got hit for speaking Spanish at school. We were learning a great deal more than was communicated by their words.

Our parents told us to listen to our teachers. The term "teacher" in Spanish, *maestro*, is a term of respect for anybody who teaches you something. Unfortunately, it was too quickly applied to those people. They weren't always the best teachers, even though it was their name and their job. And our parents got fooled as much as anybody. I don't say that with rancor. I just think it was true.

So our parents said, "Pay attention to your teachers." Our parents also taught us at home, with a belt, if I can be sort of graphic in that sense, that if you do something wrong, you're going to get hit. You're going to get punished. And so you learned that you get hit for doing something bad. And if at school you're paying attention to the teachers who say, "We're going to hit you for speaking Spanish," well, you make the mathematical leap. The mathematics of language says Spanish, then, must be bad. And there was another equation: If Spanish is bad and your parents are speaking Spanish, they must be bad people, too.

What we learned was sociology. We learned to be embarrassed of them in public. We learned to be ashamed. And we did everything we could to make sure—because we loved them—that they didn't blunder by coming out in public. We didn't let them come to PTA meetings. We didn't take the notices home. Because we loved them. We knew that if they came to school, they'd open their mouths, because that's how parents are. And because they were our parents, when they opened their mouths, they'd speak Spanish, and when they did, they'd get swatted. Now we, as second graders, thought that made sense. It was our way of taking care of them and of the world. We wanted to be good kids, and this was our way of being good.

But then, of course, somebody at the school, undoubtedly an administrator, said those Mexican parents don't care about their kids—

There you go.

They never come to meetings.

Absolutely right. Absolutely right.

Caught in the trap.

But not in the long run. It's not always as dire as it sounds. I think there were a lot of people, a lot of families, who didn't survive this. But there were many who did, who were smarter than that trap, and I think that needs to be said somewhere along the way, as well.

You have a poem called "Nani" that speaks, in some respects, about being smarter than that trap.

Let me tell you something about it. Toward the end of elementary school and the beginning of junior high school, I really couldn't speak Spanish anymore. Which is to say I learned well. I let them take it away from me.

But you can't have words taken away. They're yours forever. You can change your attitude towards them, and that's what I think happened. It wasn't until later, in high school and the beginning of college, that I re-learned Spanish. And what I was really doing was not re-learning the words at all, but re-learning my attitude toward them. Nevertheless, there was a time, late in elementary school, in particular, when I thought I couldn't speak Spanish.

My grandmother could only speak Spanish. And I was still going to her house once a week at least, for lunch, just the two of us. We had a problem. I mean, we can describe it that way. She didn't speak English. I didn't speak Spanish. But in fact, there was no problem, because we were grandmother and grandson, and what we created for ourselves was essentially another language. I don't know what to call it. It's too easy to call it the language of love or something like that. I see it as a language of some ultimate necessity. I needed her, and she needed me, and so we created for ourselves a third language, one that didn't diminish either of us. It was a simple language. It's one I think a lot of people understand. Simply, she would cook, and I would eat. And that's how we talked. It tasted good.

You've called "Nani" your breakthrough poem. Is it because, somehow, this was a poem of truth for you?

It was a poem of truth in the greater sense, in that when I wrote it, I didn't know what I was writing. It was writing me. And I think that happens sometimes with language. I wrote these words down, but I didn't "get" them.

Each time I've read "Nani," each line has come up with a kind of currency for me, a kind of meaning that is important. And I think when I realized that, I began to see that I had something in me. Maybe I didn't recognize it yet. I didn't know how to articulate it. But it was starting to come.

Has writing been for you an exploration of languages, spoken and unspoken?

Sure. And it's something bigger than that, in that it's an exploration of what languages are. I try to write to the event, to the moment. And I've come to see that language is a very poor reflection of the event. If we can stop worrying about how to say something, and look at what the thing is, we'd be in much better shape. All of us.

I think I have a playfulness of language, an awkwardness sometimes, a use of many languages at the same time in an effort to say that it's not about the language. It's about what the language is reflecting, or attempting to reflect: the event. That's what I try to get at. The heart of these things. Not the clothing that an idea wears.

Is it an attempt to bring all of life to bear on the page? And if that's so, how great a challenge is that?

It's a way of bringing one moment to bear, one moment to clarity. Drawing it up, like bringing a fish out of the water. And if you always think of it in terms of those parameters—of the single event, the single thing—trying to make that thing clear, it's not hard at all. It's not easy. It's not hard. That's the wrong measure. It's just what it is. It's just that thing you know and can talk about.

Is that poetry, for you?

It is. For me, poetry travels on a lateral plane. It's not about getting from the beginning to the end. It's about staying where you are and understanding the moment. And not being done until you essentially can show that.

Anything that propels you or compels you forward strikes

me as being troublesome. It's at the heart of everything we're seeing now in the world. All advertising, all everything makes us go forward. Clocks make us go forward. Everything says, "Keep going!" "Move!"

And that's, in some sense, what makes poetry exciting. It's outlaw-like. It's almost heresy. It's saying, "Don't go forward." Stop for a moment and understand where you're standing. Just understand this moment. I don't think you can exhaust a moment. In some curious way, I think a poem can go on forever sideways.

You can look at anything many, many, many ways. Languages show us simply alternative ways, maybe two ways, like English and Spanish. But there are many languages, and many ways to see something. And so I don't think a moment can be exhausted. I think that there's a lot there, and I don't know if that sounds deadly, this notion of non-movement, but I think there is movement. It's just lateral. It's sideways.

Burger King. Right? "Fast food for fast times!" And everybody moving to the city! And everything getting faster! We need to listen to something else. Some other message.

I don't mean this to sound too simple, but what's lost as we race forward, and what's gained if we stop?

Understanding. We know how to use things and use them well. But we don't know what they are. My favorite example is the alphabet. We use it to form words. We write sentences and paragraphs, but we build them on a foundation that we truly don't understand. We don't know what the letter *A* is anymore. *A*, going back to the Greek, is *alpha*. We say it's the beginning of the alphabet. Or it's just the beginning. Or it's a sound. Or it's a symbol. But we don't know what it's the sound of, or symbol for. In fact, it comes from the Phoenician, maybe two thousand years ago when it was upside down, a V-shape that represented the horns of an ox. An ox, for the Phoenicians, was food, and that's the first letter: food. It's the first thing. It had meaning all by itself before there were other letters. As I read it, the crossbar on the *A* was a sign that the ox was domesticated and yoked.

How did it turn itself around?

I picture a cave drawing illustrating the whole body. By the time you "wrote down" the whole ox, the ox was gone, and you didn't get to eat. So, in my way of imagining it, they used a shorthand even then: the horns. But the shorthand was asymmetrical—two horns coming to a point at the base. Human beings are particularly uncomfortable with asymmetry. So slowly—if you look at its history—the *A* starts to tumble sideways, and goes around and around until it seemingly rights itself. But, in fact, what you've got is an upside-down ox.

I think that notion of using, as opposed to understanding, is crucial. In fact, let me use one or two more examples from the alphabet. We talk a lot about sexism and racism, never considering that they're right in front of us from the moment we begin to speak. The letter *B* was originally written on its side in Phoenician. In Hebrew, it's *beth*, meaning "house." It was a drawing of a traditional Middle Eastern dwelling which had two rooms. Two very absolute, distinct rooms, one for men, one for women. Men and women were not allowed to mix because women were said to be—and this is what all the literature says—unclean. We may think that's absurd, but we continue to use the letter *B* without a thought to what it may convey from history.

My favorite is the letter *Z*. It's the sixth letter of the Greek alphabet, but it's our last letter. One of the first things you do when you conquer somebody is take away their language, because inherent in language is culture, everything about living. And when the Romans conquered the Greeks, they wanted them to become Roman, to live like them, to follow their laws. So they took their sound away. But when they used the Greeks as tutors, I can imagine the Greeks saying, "The only worthwhile literature is Greek literature. We'll teach your children, but we need our sound back to do it." And the Romans would have said, "All right, we'll let you have the letter Z—that sound—but, because it's Greek, it's going to the end of the bus, the end of the alphabet." Because it's Greek. To me that's a lesson. That's immediate. It's right in front of us. It's right there in the alphabet we use. And that's where, I think, the work of staying in place, staying with the alphabet until you understand what it is—before you start to use it—makes sense. And that "staying in place" is part of my job as a writer.

Is one of the lessons learned by the study of the alphabet, or perhaps by thinking laterally, that our histories and issues are long and deep, even in a fast-food culture? We seem to want to fix things rather quickly. We say, "Why can't people get along?" "Why can't we get rid of this prejudice?"

There's a great line by William Carlos Williams, something to the effect of, "We don't go to poems for news, yet everyday, millions die for lack of what is to be found in them."

We can learn, but we're not learning. We don't read poetry. We don't read those things that don't seem to have movement. And so I don't think we are learning from all this.

I want to ask you about the relationship between poetry and prose. You're a writer of poems that in some ways are very prose-like, and your short stories seem to emerge from poetry—sometimes literally, from particular poems.

That's right. I'm at some point of epiphany or revelation about my own work, about forms and about genre. As I'm moving toward what has traditionally been called story, I'm beginning to understand that you see poetry better in prose than you do if you go read a book of poems, where poetry is everywhere. You get inundated. You get oblivious to it. You don't recognize the moment if there are many, many moments equal to it around it. In prose, you know the poetic moment. It is blatant. It affects you. It changes how you read and how

114   *Glimmer Train Stories*

you breathe at that moment.

By the same token, I think much of poetry has lost the sense of story. And so I think my poetry has moved more towards story while my prose is moving more toward poem.

Story goes from beginning to end and gets you there. It moves. It's not lateral. It's linear. I've looked at my poems, and I'm beginning to think that's what they're doing. They have more story in them. They have more movement. They compel you increasingly forward.

My stories, though, are going more sideways. They don't offer traditional plot and structure, of going from *A* to *Z*. I think they do that ultimately, because as human beings we can't help but tell stories. We take care of ourselves by wrapping things up. We watch the letter *A* right itself, because as human beings we need the world to be right, however we measure that.

So I can start writing a story anywhere and as long as I write long enough, I will eventually tell a story. I don't think I necessarily have to impose plot, but plot I think is an organic thing. So if I begin to write a poem and I don't stop at a line break until twenty pages out, I am still writing a poem. I am truly writing a poem. It is the act of writing as an exploration, much like getting on a boat and just going with it. That's a harder, more real poem to me. What I can do in prose, or what looks like prose on the page, I'm beginning to see has more value to me as a manifestation of the poetic impulse, an exploration of the moment.

You've been doing this as writer and professor in a class you laughingly call Obsessions. But it's serious, yes?

It's very serious. I think it has transformed students. It has changed their way of thinking and of writing. It's an exciting notion. Each student comes up with one image. One student chose most recently "two people drinking from the same glass." Very simple. Just a short phrase. Each student begins with a piece of writing based on their chosen image. A poem, perhaps. They stay with the image for the rest of the semester. That's all they write about. It would seem impossible to write for three or four months about a single image. But if you can do it, the result is magical: If you can draw the rabbit out of this top hat, you will be amazed by what's possible in the world, in all those things around you.

So, we begin with the image. We extend it first backward, rather than forward, because this has to do with that temporal notion we were talking about: I don't think you should always go forward. So we go a little bit backward, to a sentence that is that image, and then to a word that is that image—not that describes the image, but is the thing. We are trying to get at what language represents. What is that image? And then we go to a letter, just as I was talking about earlier. We find a letter that is the image of two people drinking out of the same glass. It may be visual. It may have some meaning. It may be any number of things, but we find the letter that is it.

Then we go forward again. At this point it's like pulling a slingshot backward. Tension comes as you pull those rubber straps backward. When you let go of it, then you can go forward like crazy, and you've got so much farther to go if you've gone backward first. Suddenly that image has all sorts of potential. We then write it as a short story, as a prose scene, as epistolary writing, characters writing to each other. And after you've explored it, obviously you must add things, and that's what's fun. You start adding characters and setting, and it's just to accommodate the image. But in fact, you're doing all the right things you ought to do as a writer. By the end of the semester, we come back to the original form. If you wrote a poem at the beginning of the semester, then you write a poem again at the end. But the difference between those two poems, after millions of miles of exploration, is extraordinary, and it's what my students learn to call craft. That there's that much even in the single image. That, in fact, you can be a voyager of sideways.

Your own work has these powers of transformation. "The Birthday of Mrs. Piñeda," for example, began as a poem and emerged later as a short story.

And actually is evolving now into a novel. If you can't exhaust anything, it makes sense that a thing will go on. You're going to see characters in my works reappear in different settings and sometimes just in a phrase. I feel my books talk to each other, that they ought to talk to each other, that there's a sense of community here in my works, oblivious to the outside world. My books take care of each other in that way.

When "The Birthday of Mrs. Piñeda" emerged as a short story in The Iguana Killer, *it seems as if the camera was pulled back to show more of the Piñedas. The tragedy of the moment which she can never forget was not obscured, but it took its place in the house. Is this a result of writing the poem into the "poem" of the short story?*

I think it is. That notion of pulling the camera back is an excellent way to think about it. That as you go farther back, you see more, in the same way that if you begin to use more languages you understand a thing better. It is a "physicalized" language in some way. You stand back and you can say more about it.

In an essay in Ironwood *you wrote that you've always written, even as a little boy, but when you were young you "called it nothing," and you didn't tell anyone about it.*

I think if I had been writing something and I called it poetry, I might have gone to a poetry book or a poetry teacher—even though we didn't have any—but I might have tried to do that. And I think that would have been wrong. It wouldn't have been my poetry.

Could it also have been tainted by the boys on the streets? By your buddies? Was there an urge not to appear bookish?

Profound! A profound urge. It was more than not wanting to appear bookish. Whatever our perceptions are, they're strong, they're social, they're what guide us through life and let us do all those things that we do. I know that in growing up, as I was writing in the backs of my notebooks, it felt like I was getting away with something. I did homework in the front, and when I would turn my notebook to the back, I was doing what nobody had told me to do. There was no explanation for that. I was getting away with something. And I was also hiding something. Because I couldn't show it to anybody. I couldn't turn the back part of the book in to a teacher, and I didn't know what that stuff was. If I gave it no name, I also didn't know where to take it.

We didn't, in fact, have a poetry teacher. I lived in a very small town. I would call it a tough town, whatever that means. But the most immediate thing it meant to me is that if you're doing something at school that nobody tells you to do, you're different, and different isn't good to a child. And I was clearly doing something nobody else was doing. They did their homework and they were out of there—if they even did their homework. So I couldn't show it to a teacher, and neither could I show it to my friends. I'd be exposing myself in some way as something I couldn't explain even to myself. How could I explain it to them?

It's interesting that a secret became a life.

Well, I think it is.

You know, I couldn't show it to my parents, either, because kids can't do that, period. So there was some sense of hiding, and they would ask me, "Well shouldn't you be doing your homework?" It was not that I was afraid of my parents, but I knew they worried about me and what I should be doing.

As I got into high school, it's not like I couldn't figure out what I was doing, but I didn't change the mechanism. I knew that if I showed this work that—first of all, I would still be different because I was doing something others weren't doing—but if I showed it, I'd be writing, which was a curiosity, period. And I'd be writing poetry. Given the stereotypes, there was nothing to be gained. I wasn't threatened by it, but it wasn't going to help for me to show my work and to have it be labeled. If I wasn't going to use adjectives for it, I certainly wasn't going to let anybody else use adjectives for it. And so I think my writing became forcefully mine.

The short stories in The Iguana Killer *deal with what a critic called "borders." The borders between children and adults, between kids who are accepted and kids who are not. They show up in stories about the fat kid and the kid who smells funny and the kid who's flatulent and how they all learn to cope with their worlds.*

One is about youngsters on the edge of puberty—a girl who is just beginning to menstruate, and a boy who is having wet dreams. They know each other, but they don't talk because one's cool and one's not. Still, they manage, leaving notes in little pouches strung around cows' necks at the fence between them, to tell each other the most intimate details of their lives.

I'm wondering how this story came to you. Was there a basis in what we think of as the real world? Did you want to talk about secrets and how they're kept and shared?

It's all of that. I think I was every character in that story. I was the boy. I was the girl. I was the cows, too.

I was in some way trying to recover something that I felt in childhood about secrets. I think I write a great deal about secrets as well as borders. And this was an exploration of my own questions: What are my secret lives? What are my borders?

Some of it was what goes on between boys and girls. Some of it was about being a girl, or being a boy. No matter what I am as a writer, I was trying to explore those borders, to see what was there, what it meant to be on one side or the other, to be in the middle.

I am always looking for some kind of truth, though not necessarily accuracy. It didn't have to happen to me that way. It didn't all have to happen to me. Nonetheless, what I write about is all mine. It reveals a truth. But I'm not a journalist. I'm not reporting anything that happened. Still I'm talking just exactly about what happened. Picasso said, "Art is the lie that tells the truth." It follows that, in some way, ultimately, we can't lie. You know? I mean, I think I'm making this stuff up on some level or another, but I'm not. I can sort of go back and figure out why I think I invented something, where it comes from. It's just using the right ... like playing poker, you put down the right cards at the right time. And you make that happen. You make that luck, that story, that thing happen.

In "His Own Key," you take up that unabsorbable moment when a child meets up with adult information. A little boy learns from his friends how babies are born—at least he learns what they know—and is overwhelmed by that four letter word, by this new knowledge, by his disbelief and the powerful secret he now has in his mind. I would have said that here you were writing "all of life" into one moment.

It's sort of what we were saying earlier about language and meaning, and writing to the event. In this case you have more than one piece of information—the known piece and the unknown piece, the secret, and the non-secret. When you put those things together, it's like adding a set of lenses. The act brings that faraway thing, whatever it might be, closer, like binoculars. I love that. I love doing it as a writer. I love looking at the magic of binoculars. I mean, to bring a thing closer is extraordinary, and when I can do that in writing, it just makes me want to do it again.

Secrets are always on the border, on the edge. Somehow, a secret is that faraway thing that is not faraway at all. It's right in front of us, but we try to make it faraway, and there's something both right and wrong about that. I don't know which it is, but the moment you can bring that faraway thing, that secret, up close and look at it, you've done a kind of magic. It's not what the secret is about, but it's magic.

When you look into your character's confusion, you look into a very private place, but the act seems compassionate, not invasive.

I don't think I'm capable of looking at a secret and not seeing what is positive about it. That's just in my character. If I have to think about how I write, it's not to expose something that shouldn't be exposed. I just start writing about a thing, and, in the same way that plot is organic, the thing I'm writing about comes out. I don't have to impose it. I also know I'm going to take care of that secret even though I might talk about it.

In reading your short stories and your poetry, it seems you are very gentle with your characters and with your subjects.

I like them.

From the Life of Don Margarito

He was a serious man
But for one afternoon
Late in his life
With serious friends.
They adjourned to a bar
Away from the office
And its matters.
Something before dinner,
Something for the appetite
One of them had said,
And the three of them walked
In long sleeves
Into the Molino Rojo.
The cafe's twenty tables
Were pushed together
Almost entirely
Or pulled apart barely,
Giving not them
But the space between them
A dark and ragged shine
Amidst the white tablecloths.
The tables
And the spaces they made
Looked like the pieces
Of a child's puzzle
Almost done,
A continent breaking, something
From the beginning of time.
To get by them
Don Margarito had to walk
Sideways, and then sideways
Again, with arms outstretched

And up.
It was a good trick of the place
Conspiring with the music
To make the science
In this man's movement
Look like dance.

Excerpted from Ríos's new book of poems,
Two Remembered Centuries.

This interview was recorded for Conversations with Susan McInnis, KUAC-FM/TV, the University of Alaska, Fairbanks. Born in San Francisco, Susan McInnis was a producer and interviewer for public television and radio in Fairbanks for over a decade. She's now writing and editing, and on a year's leave from the far north, visiting in Sydney, Australia.

Gail Greiner

*I was very practiced in the art of being good. Here it looks
effortless, but notice the tracks of wet comb in my hair.
I must have paid dearly for those.*

This is the first short story Gail Greiner has published. She has an essay in
Child of Mine: Writers Talk About the First Year of Motherhood, edited by
Christina Baker Kline and out this spring from Hyperion.

Greiner recently finished her first year in the Columbia University School of
the Arts MFA program in writing, and lives in New York City with her
husband, her son, and their dog Rosie.

GAIL GREINER
The Croup

harlie has the croup. He woke up with a cough like a
bark and could hardly breathe. He has never had the croup
before, but I know what to do: turn on the shower and the
bath and the sink and sit with him in vapor for twenty minutes.
That should loosen it up, that should make him feel better. So
I sit on the toilet with my barking child and try not to panic.
I take deep, even breaths thinking if I slow my heartbeat, his
will slow too. As I breathe in and breathe out, Charlie's coughs
punctuate my breath. The white of the steam blends with the
white of the tiles. I have no faith that any of this will work.

We are supposed to be out at the beach tonight but our car
got towed. Earlier in the evening my husband David, and
Henry, his best friend and my lover, had taken Charlie to pick
up the car, but it was gone. We got the car last spring from two
burned-out Legal Aid lawyers who were escaping the city for
Cambodia. They gave it to us for $400. David and I named her
Katie-the-Car. We liked the alliteration and felt there was
something girlish about her. Charlie was crazy about her from
the start. We'd be out walking the dog and he'd point and say,
"Da! Da!" I'd look up and see it, a nondescript tan station
wagon with broken sidelights. Still, Katie is our wheels, Katie

is our freedom. We take her to the beach. We take her up to the fancy discount market on Friday afternoons and, when we don't have any money, charge huge amounts of groceries on my Mastercard. We buy a roasted chicken with a double side of grilled vegetables and eat it for lunch after we've put away our bounty. When we're driving in our car, under the canopy of trees on Riverside Drive, that's when I'm happiest. I'm with my family. We're in a car. We're buying groceries. These are the things I thought I'd be doing when I was married, a mother.

David opens the door to the bathroom. "What's up?" he says, squinting through the steam. And then Charlie coughs one of his coughs. "Jesus. What was that?"

"The croup," I say, irritated that he doesn't know, that he's just now waking up.

"The croup?" he says. "Good thing we didn't go to the beach."

I nod.

"You check the book?"

"Moist heat," I say, impatient. "Are you in or out? We're losing steam."

"You okay?" he asks, ready to go.

"We're fine," I say. And then, because it's too easy, I add, "Dr. Blaine."

"I've got to be up early for the salamanders," he says, apologetically. He'll go in since the beach is off.

"I know," I say. "It's fine."

He blows me a kiss without blowing it, and closes the door behind him.

David decided he wanted to be a doctor when I was exactly six weeks pregnant. "It's what I've wanted to do my whole life," he said in the bathroom one morning as I brushed my hair, his hands around my naked belly, "but it seemed impossible before this. Now everything seems possible." David used to be a painter. When we met, I was afraid to see his work, afraid of not liking it. But he took me up to the apartment he was sharing with Henry. Their dining room was David's studio. The paintings were abstract, full of color. "This is the garden out my window when I was a child," he said, pointing to one, an aerial view of splotches of red and green and yellow that could be, I saw, tomatoes and lettuce and corn. "And this is the beach where we spent our summers." The canvas was divided into silver green and crayon blue. A child's eye view of beachgrass and sky.

"What do you think?" he asked.

"They're so happy," I said. And then he led me to a painting on the other side of the dining-room table. "It's lovely," I said, looking at the undulating earthen tones, a rose glow somehow emerging behind it. "It's you," he said. And I fell in love.

I had never known David had always wanted to be a doctor. His father was a doctor. He left David's mother, a poet/ housewife, for a doctor when David was eight. When David was fifteen, his father left the first doctor for a younger doctor. Since when, I wondered, had David always wanted to be a doctor?

David majored in Fine Art so he had two years of premed requirements before he could even apply to medical school. The day we brought Charlie home from the hospital, David had his first physics class. Ten minutes before he had to leave, when we were changing Charlie, the little piece of gauze protecting his circumcision got stuck to his diaper. Charlie was screaming bloody murder and so was David. "It's okay, it's okay," I said in soothing tones as I dripped warm water from a washcloth to soften the gauze, furious I'd let them do this to my son. And then David was gone. I sat down against the door, alone for the first time with my baby, and sobbed.

"Do you not want to have this baby?" David asked as I lay

on the couch after work, flattened by nausea and overcome by the feeling that I was on a little boat, floating away from my body, my girlhood, my life. David's copy of *What to Expect When You're Expecting* lay on my alien stomach. "Depression," he read, "can lead to your not taking optimum care of yourself and your baby."

"You don't understand," I said, lifting the book and heaving it across the room. I ran into the bedroom and cried a great keening cry I had never heard come out of me before.

"It's okay, it's okay," he said, rubbing my back. "Breathe, breathe, breathe."

How could I explain to him that I did want the baby, but that I didn't want to be a mother, didn't want to be a doctor's wife. How could I explain that I was afraid that the bigger I got, the smaller I would be until I vanished.

Now Charlie is turning two and David has finished his premed requirements. He is in the waiting year. Waiting to hear about med-school interviews, waiting to find out if he is going to get in, waiting to find out where. In the meantime, he is working in a lab studying the olfactory glands of the tiger salamander. He is in charge of the care and feeding of the salamanders. He sprays their backs to keep them moist and feeds them worms. If the salamanders fall ill he puts them in the sick box, and if they get better—which rarely happens with salamanders—he transfers them to the convalescence box.

Before I saw the salamanders, I imagined them in little terrariums with greenery, sand hills, a little pond to swim in, maybe a log to hide under. But David's salamanders are kept in stacked plastic boxes, not unlike those I use for Charlie's outgrown clothes. Only these have holes punched in them.

Charlie's coughing starts up again. I wonder, not for the first time, if I should call the doctor. I'll wait the full twenty minutes, I tell myself. Because he'll ask me if I waited twenty minutes, and if I didn't, he'll just send me back to the bathroom. I do this a lot when Charlie is sick. Imagine what the doctor would say if I called. "It's going around," he'd maybe say, or, "Sounds like a virus." I imagine a virus going around like the fly in Charlie's picture book. "Old black fly's been buzzin' around, and he's had a very busy bad day." As I fight off sleep, I think about how where the fly lands is so random: on the cookies, on the keys, on the stack of clean underwear. And then I realize it's not random at all. It's not *if* he'll land on the underwear. It's when.

Tonight, when Katie was missing, Charlie was upset. He is at the stage where everything must be in order. He cannot tolerate a jacket whose zipper is not zipped up. He puts the tops back on his magic markers. He collects his pail and shovel from the sandbox before he gets out. So when he was told he and David and Henry were going to get Katie and then Katie wasn't there, this upset him. He strung together three syllables that we knew meant, "I want to drive." He pantomimed driving. He did this over and over as David called around the city to find our car and Henry stood there looking awkward. Henry did this a lot these days, whereas before he would have gone and gotten himself a beer. I wasn't thinking about Henry so much, though. I was worried about Charlie, worried that the missing car was going to be one of those seminal experiences for him, that we had compromised his sense of security. I was angry at David for not paying the parking tickets. Then Henry, still standing, looked at me with a mixture of guilt and longing. I felt like a fool.

Since I got laid off from work last year I stay home with Charlie. Occasionally I get a novelization, so I have a babysitter a couple afternoons a week. If I don't have any work I do some errands. My errands are mostly over at Henry's apartment. Henry undresses me then tucks me into bed and brings me a cup of tea which goes cold on his nightstand. At 3:45 he wakes me up, brushes my hair, and sends me home to my child. David would do these things for me, but somehow it seems more reliable that the source of this comfort is accidental.

Just when I think Charlie is calm, the cough starts up again. Last New Year's Eve our friends had a party with a palm reader. I was getting over a cold and when it was my turn, I couldn't stop coughing. "Anger," said the palm lady. "Which line is that?" I asked. I'd never heard of the anger line. "Your cough. There is something you're not saying. Anger you are leaving unexpressed. It is coming out in these spasms." I wonder if Charlie is angry.

Charlie had a preschool interview this morning. We were late for our appointment because I was supposed to bring a color Xerox of his best artwork. I had to go ten blocks out of our way so Charlie's application would be complete. During the "observed play" segment of our visit, I sat behind a one-way mirror with the headmistress and watched Charlie. He has never been an aggressive child, but I was afraid he'd choose today to hit another toddler over the head with a truck. I needn't have worried as there were no trucks and he ignored the other children. He spent most of the time in the lap of the teacher. He'd given her a book to read to him. "What's that?" asked the teacher. "Dada," said Charlie. "That's a cow," corrected the teacher. "Da!" said Charlie. "Cow," said the teacher. The headmistress scribbled in her book. After the tour, Charlie and I were invited into the headmistress's office. She held Charlie's file on her lap and paged through it slowly, reading. I had to write four essays about his development. "Salamander trainer?" she said, coming to the "occupation" slot I'd filled in under the second "parent."

"He's very good," I said.

"There is concern about Charlie's verbal skills," she said, smoothly changing the subject. "He doesn't seem attuned to the toddlers around him." She continued, "He doesn't seem to communicate with his peers."

"I didn't start talking until I was three," I said.

She stared at me with an impassive face as if to say, "And look at you."

I jerk awake. I imagine Charlie's head hitting the side of the bathtub and splitting open. I imagine hailing a cab in my white terry-cloth robe, my coughing, bleeding baby in my arms. I move from the toilet to the damp tile floor, wedging myself between the bathtub and the wall. The steam isn't as thick here, but it will have to do.

Last night David came home from his salamander lab and tried to get me to talk. All I could do was to tell him about Charlie: Charlie did x, Charlie said y. David, too, has stopped talking about himself, so he told me about his salamanders. It was feeding day, which was news of sorts, as they eat only every other week. Normally they are kept at seven degrees Celsius, but on feeding day they are warmed up so they can remember they're hungry. David has to feed each salamander by hand. They are practically blind, so they don't even know the food is in front of them until David waves the worm in their face. Then they snap. For this reason David uses tweezers to dangle the worms. "Salamanders don't have teeth," David explained, "but they can still latch on." I admire this possibility in the salamander.

David makes eight dollars an hour in the salamander lab. Most people in his position make only seven. "But," he explained, "they like me."

"The salamanders?" I asked, and I believe they do like him. He is gentle and kind and he talks to them.

"It's my confessional," he told me, but I couldn't imagine

what he confesses. Does he tell the salamanders his wife is sleeping with his best friend?

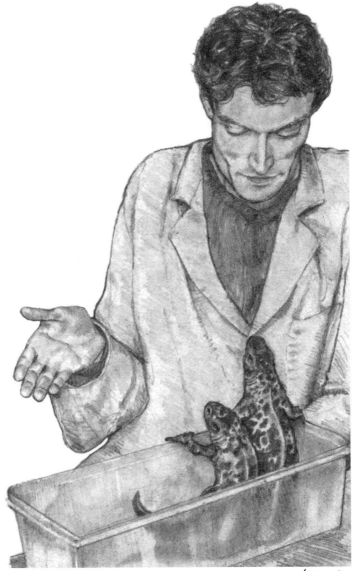

J. LEON 97-

After our interview, Charlie and I visited David at work. David was busy showing Charlie his salamanders. I imagined they were looking at me. "Whore," said one. "Bitch," said another. "Ungrateful," said a third. "Just wait 'til he's gone," crooned a fourth. "Then she'll be alone. She'll die penniless and alone in the Chelsea Hotel."

"That's enough," I said out loud.

"I know, it's cold in here," said David, grabbing my hand and Charlie's, leading us out, closing the meat-locker door behind us.

"The salamanders know," I said to Henry this afternoon, sitting up and pulling on my shirt.

"Did you tell them?" he asked as he nuzzled my neck.

"No, David did."

"You don't think David knows, do you?" he said looking at me.

"It depends on what you mean by 'know.'"

In the bathroom, I awake drooling, my neck kinked. I have been dreaming that the croup is feathers, tiny chicken feathers lodged in the esophagus. In my dream, Charlie started coughing them up, downy feathers. Charlie wakes up now, but he's not coughing feathers. He's not coughing at all, though he does start to cry. Sitting in the half-mist on the floor, my back against the tub, my feet against the wall, I part my robe so he can press his damp cheek against my bare skin. He quiets instantly. I stopped nursing months ago, yet still my breasts have the ability to comfort him. I think about the magical power of the breast, how it can feed and pacify and excite. I think how ironic, and really how perfectly circular, that under its milky skin, in its cauliflower ducts and glands, it can also harbor death.

Henry was only dropping the keys off that first time, telling me where the car was parked. "On the building side of the drive," he said, "just below the fireman's memorial." He did this all the time, borrowed the car to take on one of his jobs, stashing his boom and his box and his other soundman equipment in the roomy back of our funky wagon. "Hey, thanks guys," he would say at the door at the end of his day, grateful for the use of the car, not taking it for granted, offering to pay to replace the timing belt. But on that one night, David wasn't home and I had been crying. It had only been a few months since my mother died, and in the particular world created by the birth of a child, the nursing and swaddling and changing and holding and loving this infant, I had not mourned.

Henry stood in the doorway with his big black bag slung over his shoulder. "Hey," he said, "are you okay?" And then, of course, I cried some more. He put down his bag and followed me to the couch where I sat and put my face in my hands and apologized, and he sat, too. I looked at him and said, "I'm so sorry," and he said, "It's okay," and, as if to emphasize his words, he leaned over and kissed me, and I kissed him back. I felt a kind of window open up out of my sorrow, and I forgot I was a motherless mother. For that moment I was only light and space and air.

"Hey." It is David through the steam. "He's asleep."

I have somehow managed to curl up on the floor. The baby is in a nest of towels. He is breathing slowly, evenly, quietly.

I raise myself on one arm.

"Your skin is all rosy," David says, looking at me after turning off the water. A heavy slice of paint falls from the ceiling.

"Lead?" I ask, too tired to care.

"Probably," he says. "We'll clean it up in the morning. Come on." He scoops up Charlie and holds him in the crook of his arm. He puts out his other hand.

"You sleep tomorrow," he says. "The salamanders will live."

"But I don't want them to live," I say.

And then I sleep.

Michael Byers

*Singing with my buddy Mel Wax, in the days
when toys were bigger than me.*

Michael Byers grew up in Seattle, where many of his stories take place. His
fiction has appeared in the *Missouri Review, American Short Fiction*, and other
magazines, and has been included in *Prize Stories 1995: The O. Henry Awards*
and *Best American Short Stories 1997*. His book of stories, *The Coast of Good
Intentions*, will be published in April by Houghton Mifflin. He is a Stegner
Fellow at Stanford and lives in San Francisco.

MICHAEL BYERS
Dirigibles

*H*oward and Louise walked arm-in-arm down the
tilted field, and when they were forty feet from the beehives
they stopped, because at this point Louise was usually tired, and
because Howard knew this was really as close as Louise liked
to get. She leaned heavily on Howard's arm, breathing. It was
August, so it was warm in the dry field, and a flat mountain heat
rose from the grass.

She said, "Just a minute."

"Yep," Howard said.

She arched her back and cleared her throat, and sighed. She
was a short, round woman with gray hair and a prominent
nose, and she'd been sick for some time with multiple sclerosis;
these days she found it difficult to walk. Her clavicle stood out
under her clothes like a handle, and her feet were long and
narrow in their gray sneakers. For a long moment they stood
together in the field. Around them, in the deep, late-afternoon
light, Howard could see his bees—they hovered here and there
over the pasture, like a handful of pebbles that had been tossed
into the air and hadn't come down.

"I'll just wait," she said, "over here." She leaned against the
fence.

Glimmer Train Stories, Issue 26, Spring 1998
©1997 Michael Byers

Howard picked up his things and went off toward the beehives. He worried about his wife; even on her good days she was tiring more easily. It was hard to see unless you'd been with her a long time, but he could see it.

At the beehives Howard pulled on his gloves and lowered his helmet onto his head; then he knelt, and, carefully, as though sliding delicate mail out of a box, pulled out a long shelf of bees. They crawled earnestly over his gloves, up and down his stubby fingers, hundreds of them, little balls of yellow thread that ambled around the frame of the shelf and flew off aimlessly, looping around his head, landing on his plastic helmet. He loved them for the dependable way they flew out and back every day; they were admirable things, he thought. He liked the sweet, electric smell of the bees, too, an odor that rose now from the dark interior of the hive. He pushed them delicately off his gloves and collected a jarful of honey, and when he slid the shelves back in, a few bees went shooting away over the field. He walked back to his wife, carrying the jar, which was warm in his hand.

"They gave me a deal," he said, holding it up. "Half off."

"You've got a bee in there."

"Ah-ha," he said. He reached in and scooped it out, dead, with his finger, and wiped it on the grass. "So they sold me a bill of goods."

They walked back up toward the house. Their long shadows stretched in front of them. His old rounded tractor lay under a tarp in a corner of the field, and their house, an A-frame he had built himself, stood at the top of the field, high and triangular against the dark woods. He'd been very organized in his life, Howard had, but recently he had begun to let things go. He hadn't looked at the tractor in months, and he'd almost forgotten it was there. He had been forgetting lots of things lately, and it frightened him to feel like this, as though it were all very decisively beginning to come apart. They didn't answer the phone sometimes, and that bothered him, too; after it stopped ringing and the house was quiet again, he felt as though a big hole had been torn in the day. Not that it was ever anyone important. Their kids never called. But it was unsettling, as though they had decided to step aside from things.

Louise let go of his arm. She walked along beside him, lifting one narrow foot out of the grass, then the other. After a minute of this she came back and took up his arm again.

"I'm not looking forward to tonight," she said.

"He's a nice guy. You remember him."

"No, I don't," she said. "I don't remember him at all."

"We'll stay out of your way, if you want."

"Well." She lifted the hem of her dress and examined her sneakers. "By all means, don't mind me."

James Couch, a friend of theirs from the old days, was coming to dinner, driving over from Seattle and then leaving again the next morning—he would stay in a motel—on his way to Montana to see his daughter. Howard and James Couch had worked together on the ferries in Seattle years ago. Howard had been a ferry captain, and James Couch had worked alongside him, his first mate, for three years, before Couch got his own boat. Really they hadn't been all that close, Howard hadn't liked making friends at work, but Howard and Louise didn't have many friends anymore, so Howard didn't feel he could be choosy.

Howard set up his film projector in the living room and stacked his film cans like thick, impossible coins beside it. Then, after assuring himself it was entirely clean, he tacked a white sheet to the living room wall. He had movies of the ferry days, which he supposed James Couch would like; Howard himself hadn't seen them in years. He'd more or less forgotten what was on them.

"Oh, Howard, not those," Louise said, peering in, examining the labels.

"Why not?"

"Show him some slides or something."

"He's my friend," Howard said, "and I'll show him what I want."

"Of course you don't remember what's on those."

"Of course I do."

"Well," Louise said, and shrugged. "Okey dokey." She hobbled out of the room.

So Howard waited. He sat on the porch in a lawn chair. He opened a bottle of beer and drank it slowly, watching the sun setting behind the trees. A hummingbird approached the porch, then darted away. They'd been lucky to get the place when they had, twenty years ago, when no one wanted to live here on the hot, unsophisticated side of the mountains; they'd ended up with a lot of land they couldn't possibly have afforded if they were buying today. Now there were espresso stands in town, even here, run by girls in green aprons—he wouldn't have thought it, but Howard actually liked driving down to town in the mornings and getting two coffees and bringing them back with the paper. It was a small life and he thought a good one. They'd planted a row of apple trees and grew their own vegetables, and now that he had retired from the ferries, they lived here from March to October, returning to their little house in Seattle just as the rainy season started, avoiding the snow that fell heavily here in Roslyn. Howard liked the snow, but it was hard to get around in, especially with Louise.

Howard didn't mind his wife's illness, not exactly, though he would never have said as much out loud—in fact he mostly enjoyed taking what care of her he could. It wasn't much. She had her good days and bad. He vacuumed now, which he'd never done before. He did the laundry. He'd traded in their stick shift for an automatic, because Louise couldn't use the clutch anymore, and every morning in the city he got on his bony ten-speed bicycle and rode around the lake for exercise, admiring his tall, long-legged shadow, like a spider under his black helmet. His knees ached and yellow spots flashed in his eyes when he climbed the hills, but on he went. He loved his wife, and this fact made him feel good; but she unnerved him a little, too. My leg, she might say, I can't move my leg. And they'd both look at it there, under her hands.

A car appeared at the bottom of the pasture and made its way slowly up the road, bucking and tossing. It was an old rusty car the color of grass, with a luggage rack on top. Howard went inside and put his bottle in the sink. "He's here."

"Oh, Jesus." Louise closed the refrigerator with the rubber tip of her cane. "He's early."

Before he opened the front door Howard wiped his hands on his pants, pushed his hair back with two hands, and smoothed down his shirt.

The car pulled up to the house, and James Couch got out and stretched. He wore a thin white sweater and blue jeans; he was a short man with a white beard and a thick torso, and he was bald, the smooth dome of his head rising like something architectural. He came bounding up the steps and shook Howard's hand vigorously, nodding in time. His papery scalp stretched tight over the top of his head.

"Howard," he said.

"Hiya. Been a while."

"How've you been?"

"We've been okay."

"Louise's here?"

"You bet," Howard said. "Come on in."

James Couch leaned toward him and took his elbow, gently. Couch's white beard shone on his face; it was woven through with black hairs, and looked infinitely soft. "I have something for you," Couch said.

"Okay."

"I'll give it to you later," Couch said, and patted his pocket. "I want to see Louise first."

They went indoors and found Louise in the kitchen. She shook James Couch's hand. "You're a little early."

"Sorry," Couch said. "I didn't know where you were so I gave myself a little extra time. In case I missed a turn somewhere."

"Well. No harm done." She pressed his hand hard, with both of hers. "We get lonely up here. We don't like to admit that, but it's true."

"We don't get lonely," Howard said.

"Yes, we do, Howard."

"No we don't," he said.

"It's beautiful up here," Couch said.

Louise smiled and widened her eyes. "Yes it is. We forget about that sometimes. Come out on the porch."

They walked back out to the porch together. The air was cool outside, and smelled like dry grass and the dark, intricate depths of the woods. The mountains stood silhouetted against the green sky, and at the bottom of the pasture they could see the beehives, tall white boxes, luminous in the dusk.

Louise said, "It's hard to see it sometimes, when you see it every day."

Couch nodded, taking in the scenery. "You know, I went to Iceland this summer," he said. "Ever been there?"

"No," Howard said.

His wife said, "I suppose it's beautiful."

"Oh, hell yes. *Hell* yes. I was up there this summer, on

vacation, you know, and what happens when I get there but there's this volcano going off, if you can believe it."

"Oh, for heaven's sake," Louise said.

"Yes. A thing to see. Steam everywhere. Lava going into the ocean, you know, really spectacular. Huge. You could see it for miles. Miles."

"What a coincidence," Louise said. "Good timing for you."

"Yes, it was. Yes indeed." He reached into his pants pocket and took out a rock. It was an ordinary flat stone from the bottom of a river, smooth and black, with a white vein running through it. He held it out and gave it to Louise. "This is a piece of lava," he said. "From the volcano."

Louise took it, turned it over once in her palm. "Well," she said. "It's lovely."

"A brand new rock. Five weeks old."

"*That* rock is?" Howard said.

"Howard," said Louise, "isn't it lovely?" She held it out to him, and Howard took it from Louise's palm and felt it, heavy and cool, then handed it back to her.

"You got that in Iceland?" Howard asked. It was ridiculous. But Couch wasn't kidding.

"Keep it. I've got a dozen. We were living in the crater, you know. It was spectacular. Like being in the middle of a movie. Rocks just flying everywhere."

"Living in the crater?" Howard said.

"Yep. For a month we lived in the crater. They had a motel there."

"A motel?"

"Yes, we were guests of the state. They needed volcano experts."

"You don't say," Howard said.

Louise turned the rock over. "It's very thoughtful of you," she said, and touched Howard's hand, then took her hand back. "We'll put it in a special place. Thank you."

"It is my genuine pleasure." He smoothed his hand over his scalp. "I liked you guys a whole lot. You were the reason I stayed on at the ferries for as long as I did." He paused for a moment and then said, with great feeling, "*Iceland.*"

Far away, they could see a sprinkling of lights at the bottom of the hill; this was Roslyn, the town. Howard imagined what was happening there now, the pickups, the Dairy Queen full of teenagers. It was a pleasant thought, the idea of life going on elsewhere. He thought about James Couch, too, but it wasn't much of a thought, and it amounted to this: James Couch wasn't the man he had been. Or maybe that was putting it generously. Really what Howard thought, though he knew it wasn't very polite, was this: James Couch had gone a little way around the bend, and he wasn't coming back.

At dinner, Louise said, "I don't remember you talking about your daughter."

"My daughter." Couch nodded. "My daughter is something to talk about. Now she—*she* is an adventurer." He ate quite normally, Howard noticed; he drank his beer out of a glass, which Howard himself never did. He didn't eat too quickly, or too slowly. He chewed with his mouth closed. When he had food in his beard, he knew it, and wiped it away. He was handsome, Howard supposed, in a sort of nautical way, with the beard and the sweater.

"What's your daughter's name?" Howard asked.

"Deedee. Deedee is a hang glider."

"Is that so," Louise said.

"Yes it is. She's a daredevil."

"Good for her," Louise said.

"She goes up in the mountains and off she goes. Beautiful. She was telling me," Couch said, and pushed his chair back a little, "she got caught the other day in this updraft, she was over a hot spot, or however it is, you know, an upwelling, and she

144   *Glimmer Train Stories*

couldn't get out of it, and she just kept going up, up, up, up."
His flat hand rose slowly from the dinner table, tipping, and
Howard watched it, entranced. "She couldn't do a thing. She
just kept going up."

"Uh-oh," Howard said.

"You bet your life uh-oh."

Louise said, "It must have been terrifying for her."

"Well. So what happened was," Couch said, "she goes up
and up, and just keeps going, and finally she just goes out into
outer space. Breaks right through the top of the atmosphere
and she's just out there."

Howard cleared his throat. "In outer space?"

"My goodness," Louise said. "Imagine that."

"Luckily she made it back," Couch said. "But she's sort of
shied off the hang gliding a little bit since then."

"I bet," Howard said.

"You can't blame her," Couch said.

"No, I guess not," Howard said.

"That must have been a wonderful trip," Louise said. "How
beautiful, to be up so high."

"Like I say," Couch said, "she is an adventurer."

At some point during dinner, Louise squeezed Howard's
knee once, hard, and smiled at him. Her hair was pinned back
behind her neck. She sat square to the table, with authority.
She'd worked on the ferries for years, too, throwing out ropes,
pulling ropes in, waving cars down the banging ramps.

When Couch went to the bathroom, Louise said, quietly,
"So?"

Howard shrugged. "Got me."

"I don't think he should drive to Montana like that."

"Well, I don't know. He got here okay."

"I think he should stay with us tonight," she said. "We'll
figure something out in the morning."

MICHAEL BYERS

"Well," Howard said, "okay. We'll put him upstairs." They had a spare bedroom in the attic.

They sat together, listening to James Couch pee in the bathroom.

After a minute, Louise said, "You know, he's wonderful." She touched her fork, her knife. "I had no idea."

"I think what he is is crazy."

Louise lifted her arms into the air, embracing nothing. "I want to *keep* him," she said.

After dinner was cleared, they decided to watch the movies.

"This should be good," Louise said.

"Hell yes," James Couch said. "Put 'em on." He got up and began rearranging the furniture. Louise sat apologetically in her chair, not helping, every now and then taking a breath as though to speak. Couch in his white sweater lifted the living-room chairs higher than he had to, and set them down with ostentatious care.

The strip of film was old, narrower than Howard remembered; it smelled flat and clean, like old tape. He threaded the film up and around, through the projector, and then turned on the motor and the lamp. Immediately there was the hot smell of burning dust and the whirring sound of the film racheting through its rounds, curling up and around and gathering on the takeup reel.

Howard aimed and focused and, all at once, there he was on the white sheet on the wall, much younger, tragically younger, his face fuller and brighter, his arms stronger. His young hair whipped in the wind. He was on a ship, and behind him was a view of the sea, the open sea, and the ship was rocking slightly. But these weren't the ferry movies; these were his Navy movies.

"These are the wrong movies," Howard said.

"That's all right."

"These are my Navy movies. You won't recognize any of these people."

"Oh, that's okay. I don't mind."

"Well," Howard said, "that's Alaska." He found it difficult to speak. There he was. A shot of a group of men, their hair cut astronaut-short. They were tanned, shirtless. They waved. He was among them, the tall, loose-jointed one in back, the one not wearing sunglasses. A boat was lowered into the water and motored away. Two men in wetsuits appeared from below the surface of the water, and lifted their masks. A dark view of something that might have been a sunset.

He read the lid of the film can. "I guess this is 1957."

A mountain slid by, followed by a shot of the empty deck. Then a shot of the galley, where men squinted into the camera's obvious light, holding up their hands to shade their eyes. Another set of divers dropped abruptly into the water and sank.

"Daily life."

The screen went dark; then came a shot of the outside of their house in Seattle. The lawn was kept as it always was: their old Valiant sat at the curb, looking fierce and cantilevered, fins rising over the taillights.

"Oh, the Valiant," Louise said.

Then Howard remembered this particular reel of film.

The wall went dark again. Next there came the inside of their Seattle house, the back hall. There stood the table, in its place; there was the old carpet, the old dark ceiling. Then, in the darkness, a figure appeared. It was Louise, naked, running from one doorway to another, the briefest of pictures. She was young and thin, and almost all leg, or her legs were the brightest part of her, flashing when they scissored their way across the hallway and disappeared. Her torso was vaguer, darker. The shape of a small breast was fleetingly visible, the side of her face a smudge. But it was her.

J.LEON 97-

Then the screen flashed a brilliant light, and the reel was over. Nobody said anything for a minute.

"Well," Louise said, stomping her cane on the carpet. "That would be me."

Howard turned on a floor lamp and switched off the projector. "Well, well," he said. He laughed, and Louise laughed, too. James Couch rubbed a flat hand over his bald head and tried to smile, but he couldn't manage it, quite; he tipped his head to one side and looked at the floor. Howard remembered it now: he'd come home after three months, a sailor, and Louise had surprised him, appeared naked at the door, taken his bags, offered to make him coffee, all as if nothing were unusual. He'd taken the camera from his backpack, gone back outside, shot the house, the car, just as he had seen them, then used the last of the film on her. He felt a surge of real happiness at the memory. He was almost sixty-seven, she was sixty-eight, but it didn't matter. They had been together all their lives, or near enough. All this should have

148   *Glimmer Train Stories*

made him afraid, he thought, afraid of dying at least, but he wasn't afraid, or at least not now, not on this hill, in this house. Nothing could make him afraid.

Louise, giggling, got up and turned on the dishwasher. Howard put the film chastely back into its tin container. Outside, the wind began to blow. Couch sat still for a moment longer, then stood up and began putting the furniture back where it belonged. He reached up and unpinned the sheet, folding it once, twice, then again, then hanging it over his arm, as a waiter would.

Howard opened the attic-bedroom door. The roof here met at a peak; the walls were bare wood, dark old cedar. In the room were a white metal bed, a white dresser, and an oval rug, all undisturbed for months. Above the bed was a small rectangular window, about the size of a magazine, that gave a view on darkness. It was cold in the room, but there were blankets.

"This should hold you," Howard said, and took blankets off the dresser.

James Couch nodded, watching him placidly. "I really appreciate this," he said.

"That's a long drive you've got tomorrow."

"I know it."

"You need your sleep."

Couch helped spread the blankets over the bed. Then he said, "I can hardly remember us from before."

Howard tucked in the blankets. "We're just getting older."

"Maybe so."

Howard fluffed Couch's pillows. "If there's anything you need," Howard said, when he was done, "just knock on our door. You know which one it is."

"Okay."

"There's only the one bathroom."

"That's okay. I can manage."

Howard couldn't think of anything more to say, but he didn't want to go. He stood there for a long while, watching Couch rearrange the pillows and smooth out the last of the blankets. At last Howard said, "Maybe you'll think about staying on a little bit tomorrow. I wouldn't mind at all."

"I really have to get back on the road."

"You'll stay for breakfast, at least. I'll show you my beehives."

"Sure. I'd like that." Couch felt his white beard and sat down on the bed. He began taking off his shoes. "I really do appreciate this," he said again.

"You bet. Any time." When Howard left him, James Couch was sliding his shoes carefully under the bed, first one, then the other.

Downstairs, Howard washed his face with an old, thin washcloth. The cloth came away gray, and his hands, when he washed them, ran gray water down the sink. The wind had increased and now blew with some force across the chimney top. The house in its stand of trees was shut up tight, locked, and Louise was down the hall, in bed. Howard turned out the kitchen light. Conscious of his footsteps on the cold floor, he stepped softly, though he couldn't think why. From beneath their bedroom door a crack of light showed; Louise looked up from her book when he came in. Her hair hung over her shoulders. Howard loosened his belt and slid his pants to the floor. He opened one of the windows above their bed. In the backyard the fir trees bent as air swooshed through them. He'd spent so many years on the water, he thought.

Louise said, "Come to bed."

He climbed under the covers.

Louise kept reading. He turned on his bedside light and picked up a magazine. He read for a while, listening to the wind and feeling it on his cheek, just a little too cold. Their feet touched under the blankets, then moved apart again.

150

"He's okay?" she asked.

"He's okay."

She said, after a minute, "The poor man."

Howard listened for noise from the attic, but there wasn't any.

"He must have been wonderful," she said.

"You don't remember him."

"No," she said.

Outside, the wind kept moving toward them over the fields, up the valley, and it filled Howard's heart as though his heart were a sail. Needles fell from the trees to the earth. The magazine fluttered in his hands, turning its own pages.

After a long while Howard said, quietly, "You know I played the greatest concert halls in Germany before the war."

Louise turned a page. After a moment she said, "I never knew that."

"I ran in the highest circles of power," he said. "I was master among men."

"Oh, Howard," she said. "I had no idea."

"Ten thousand women waited on my every need."

"Really," she said.

"My name in lights around the world."

"Imagine," she said.

"Think of me like that."

"Yes."

"I flew in the great dirigibles of the age," said Howard.

"Yes, you must have."

"Flew over all the great nations of the earth."

"Yes, I know."

"Rivers and plains beneath me."

"Yes."

"It's true," Howard said. "Everything is true."

"Oh, Howard," Louise said, and closed her book. "Howard."

The Last Pages

Oscar Ebe and his dog, 1918

*T*his is Irene and Arthur Gross, circa 1958 in New York City. Both are from sophisticated families in Poland. Before World War II, Arthur was a boxer and member of the Polish army. Irene was a pianist. They were married in the Warsaw ghetto in 1940. Shortly afterwards they were placed in concentration camps, and separated for three years. After the Liberation, they were reunited through the actions of a boy whose life Irene had saved. Arthur Gross and Irene Zimer were the sole surviving members of each of their families. In 1949, they arrived in America.

I married their oldest daughter, Rita Lily Gross, in 1987. I was unemployed, non-urban, and poorly educated. I wanted to be a writer without having published anything. I was also not Jewish. These were grave concerns of mine at the time. I was deeply afraid that Rita's parents would disapprove of me. Instead, they took me in like a son, and taught me about acceptance, forgiveness, compassion, and love.

GAIL GREINER

*W*hen I was in college, Grace Paley came to speak about writing. I asked her what advice she had for women trying to write in the midst of raising children. "Use it," she said. "The Croup" was the first story I wrote at Columbia. I had a story due in a week, I hadn't written a word, and my son had been up coughing five nights in a row. Desperate for sleep, wired on Diet Coke, I started pounding on my computer:

"I'm all blocked and afraid and I feel like I'm getting a sore throat and I don't know how I'm going to write this story and N. has been sick for five days and I'm exhausted and the paint is falling in big chunks from the ceiling and the car got towed ..."

Something clicked then, and I just kept writing. Thank you, Grace Paley. And thanks to Helen Schulman for encouraging me to take it to the next level.

154

DANIEL VILLASENOR

I have an unreproducible picture of a turn-of-the-century blacksmith shop in Bozeman, Montana, where I went to study the trade. It was gifted to me by the man who first taught me the work. There are three men in the picture: a smith standing behind the anvil, a striker (one who swings the heavy sledge), and a loafer with a mug in his hand who looks, appropriately, quite like Walt Whitman, though he was probably old enough to be his father. Evidently these fellows were deeply skilled: they were wheelwrights, too—you can see the wheel leaning in what looks like a doorway in sunlight. And they shod horses—the shoes are hanging under the tongs by the brick coal forge. What I like about it is that nothing's changed: the swedge block, the anvil, the sledge, tongs, and hotcut—it's not different today, and it was no different a hundred years before the picture was taken. But more, there's a mood to the men, a look of irascible impatience at photography itself, as if the freezing of time is incommensurate with labor, which it probably is. I've come to see that look as admonitory, as a figure for the privileged remove art can sometimes be.

I once told a writer, a stranger, that I was a blacksmith, and he said such a job must be great material for writing. But that's not it; that's an insult to the trade. Not that he meant it to be—he was a nice, well-meaning guy. But the trade is a life unto itself, material or no. In the story, Wendell happens to work with metal, but he's not a blacksmith, and there's a big difference between a welder and a blacksmith. It's more the immemorial craft, the horses and the forge and the steel and a quality of physical exhaustion at the end of the day, which gives me permission to try and tell stories. So that guy wasn't far off. In some bedrock sense, regardless of subject matter, I owe this story, and all those to come, to the trade.

Photo credit Dwight Flowers

I grew up in a *rashomon*. My mother and her sister married my father and his brother; both couples divorced after having children. This is what made my childhood unique and forged me as a writer—so many voices and versions surrounding a common event, a polyphony I heard inside as well as outside, because I was always caught in the middle and would grant each relative his or her wish to have the one true version.

My characters' natural empathy gets them into trouble. They are mistaken for other people's loved ones; they mistake others for their own loved ones. I write about people who have few family ties and doubt their own ability to make them. They are drawn to families that are already formed. This is true of the narrator of "One of Me Watching." Her mother has found the man she wants to marry but Frances is left wondering if this is a family to which she can belong. As a writer, I'm interested in a specific generation—people who have gone from multiple parents to multiple partners. I'm not sure that such a history makes it any easier for people to choose each other.

When I wrote this story, I did some medical research about brain hemorrhages. Anders is the only character I made up entirely. The others are composites from my travels. When I submitted this story in an earlier form to a graduate-school workshop, many students said they wished the other characters were as real as Anders. That pleased me. I could trust my imagination.

With my son, Connor, the bug (age five).

I have no idea where this story comes from. I have never driven a De Soto, nor cashed a second-party check for $54,000.

The apprenticeship of a writer is completely promiscuous. You inhale the universe and then—minutes, days, or years later—you exhale and are surprised at what comes out.

In the sixties I drove a cab in New York City. Unlike the President, I inhaled a lot during those years. "Closure" floated to the surface some twenty-seven years later. It probably has nothing to do with driving a cab. But then it may have everything to do with it. I just don't know.

TAXICAB DRIVER'S LICENSE
EXPIRES MAY 31, 1969

PETER
LEFCOURT
37182

YOU MUST RENEW THIS LICENSE BETWEEN

POLICE DEPARTMENT
CITY OF NEW YORK

Portrait of the Artist as a Young Cab Driver

MICHAEL BYERS

A friend recently noticed that my stories were often about older people, and was wondering why. I didn't really know why. "Dirigibles" started out as a story called "Noah," in which Howard and Louise were actually much younger. In this story, their son Dale comes home to announce his marriage. The son, a sort of beet-faced guy, didn't wear well, and Howard was grumpy and unhappy, and so was Louise. The whole thing got chucked and when the story came out of the drawer again, years later, all that remained were Howard's bees. The son was nowhere in sight. Then James Couch arrived, and things were on the right track. Howard got older and more hopeful. Louise did too. The two of them came to a place in their lives, I guess, where happiness could arrive from any direction. The story, having changed so much, now feels to me like a last chapter of something much longer. I'm pleased to see the two of them at peace together here. And I think that may be why I like stories about older people; I like knowing how things turn out.

*P*AST CONTRIBUTING AUTHORS AND ARTISTS
Issues 1 through 25 are available for eleven dollars each.

Robert H. Abel • Linsey Abrams • Steve Adams • Susan Alenick • Rosemary Altea • Julia Alvarez • A. Manette Ansay • Margaret Atwood • Aida Baker • Brad Barkley • Kyle Ann Bates • Richard Bausch • Robert Bausch • Charles Baxter • Ann Beattie • Barbara Bechtold • Cathie Beck • Kristen Birchett • Melanie Bishop • Corinne Demas Bliss • Valerie Block • Joan Bohorfoush • Harold Brodkey • Danit Brown • Kurt McGinnis Brown • Paul Brownfield • Judy Budnitz • Evan Burton • Gerard Byrne • Jack Cady • Annie Callan • Kevin Canty • Peter Carey • Brian Champeau • Carolyn Chute • George Clark • Dennis Clemmens • Evan S. Connell • Wendy Counsil • Toi Derricotte • Tiziana di Marina • Junot Díaz • Stephen Dixon • Michael Dorris • Siobhan Dowd • Barbara Eiswerth • Mary Ellis • James English • Tony Eprile • Louise Erdrich • Zoë Evamy • Nomi Eve • Edward Falco • Michael Frank • Pete Fromm • Daniel Gabriel • Ernest Gaines • Tess Gallagher • Louis Gallo • Kent Gardien • Ellen Gilchrist • Mary Gordon • Peter Gordon • Elizabeth Graver • Paul Griner • Elizabeth Logan Harris • Marina Harris • Erin Hart • Daniel Hayes • David Haynes • Ursula Hegi • Amy Hempel • Andee Hochman • Alice Hoffman • Jack Holland • Noy Holland • Lucy Honig • Ann Hood • Linda Hornbuckle • David Huddle • Stewart David Ikeda • Lawson Fusao Inada • Elizabeth Inness-Brown • Andrea Jeyaveeran • Charles Johnson • Wayne Johnson • Thom Jones • Cyril Jones-Kellet • Elizabeth Judd • Jiri Kajanë • Hester Kaplan • Wayne Karlin • Thomas E. Kennedy • Jamaica Kincaid • Lily King • Maina wa Kinyatti • Carolyn Kizer • Jake Kreilkamp • Marilyn Krysl • Frances Kuffel • Anatoly Kurchatkin • Victoria Lancelotta • Doug Lawson • Don Lee • Jon Leon • Doris Lessing • Janice Levy • Christine Liotta • Rosina Lippi-Green • David Long • Salvatore Diego Lopez • William Luvaas • Jeff MacNelly • R. Kevin Maler • Lee Martin • Alice Mattison • Eileen McGuire • Gregory McNamee • Frank Michel • Alyce Miller • Katherine Min • Mary McGarry Morris • Bernard Mulligan • Abdelrahman Munif • Kent Nelson • Sigrid Nunez • Joyce Carol Oates • Tim O'Brien • Vana O'Brien • Mary O'Dell • Elizabeth Oness • Karen Outen • Mary Overton • Patricia Page • Peter Parsons • Steven Polansky • Annie Proulx • Jonathan Raban • George Rabasa • Paul Rawlins • Nancy Reisman • Linda Reynolds • Anne Rice • Roxana Robinson • Stan Rogal • Frank Ronan • Elizabeth Rosen • Janice Rosenberg • Kiran Kaur Saini • Libby Schmais • Natalie Schoen • Jim Schumock • Barbara Scot • Amy Selwyn • Catherine Seto • Bob Shacochis • Evelyn Sharenov • Ami Silber • Floyd Skloot • Gregory Spatz • Lara Stapleton • Barbara Stevens • William Styron • Liz Szabla • Paul Theroux • Abigail Thomas • Randolph Thomas • Joyce Thompson • Patrick Tierney • Andrew Toos • Patricia Traxler • Christine Turner • Kathleen Tyau • Michael Upchurch • Daniel Wallace • Lance Weller • Ed Weyhing • Joan Wickersham • Lex Williford • Gary Wilson • Terry Wolverton • Monica Wood • Christopher Woods • Celia Wren • Brennen Wysong • Jane Zwinger

Harry and Lina Wyman, 1927

Coming soon:

Tom reached over to the passenger seat and ran his hand along the well-worn black leather upholstery—a network of grey lines that each seemed to tell a story, like those on an old man's face. He felt very affectionate toward his car, which was, besides clothing, the only possession he had held on to through his last three marriages.

from "Angel" by Jenny Drake McPhee

Now Tyler's picture of the world and his sense of mastery over it were quietly exploded. His new employer was a young company looking for contracts in overseas markets off the beaten path, and Tyler found himself going to Borneo, Chile, Saudi Arabia, and, in early 1985, Johannesburg.

from "The Cave" by Michael Upchurch

General Mersh returned from the Crimea whole and well. The only immediate indication of his participation in war and battle was the stain on his tunic.

from "The Stain" by Richard Lyons

At least one of his more questionable visions had turned out to be real. What did that tell him? That which is seen out of the corner of one's eye may not be a trick of the light; that which is invisible may be that which is simply able to hide; that which may seem a ghost may be many different things, only one of which is a fantasy, a falsehood, a failure of the mind.

from "Keeper" by Steve Adams

160

MAY 3 0 2024